YOU'VE GOT BOOKMAIL

LEYA LAYNE

Trigger Warnings

While this book is meant to be a quick, fun romance with lots of spice, there are discussions of topics that could be triggering for readers. To be respectful to those who need warnings and those who see them as spoilers, I have placed the trigger warnings on my website. Scan this code to check the site.

ACKNOWLEDGMENTS

I've heard it said, and I truly believe, that inspiration can come from anywhere. This time, it came from a simple TikTok video where one of my mutuals asked for a romance novel with a male love interest in uniform that isn't the expected military or police uniform. Her next request was for the female main character to be a book lover. Kassandra and Asher developed from these thoughts, and I've had so much fun writing them. So, thank you Sarah for your video and your dedication to books.

I also want to acknowledge my writing crew who keep me sane and pushing to make this writing thing more than I could have ever imagined. Thank you, Britton, Ashley, and Gracie for the friendships we've built and the delusions we share.

Last, but certainly not least, a huge thank you to Darrelle for all the home improvement shows and dreams for the future. Your belief in my writing ability is the whole reason I'm here.

CHAPTER 1
KASSANDRA

S har lounged on the chaise with a fluffy romance novel in her hand watching him surf the waves. She brought the book because she thought the day would be boring without something spicy to stimulate her mind. Ok, maybe there was more she wanted stimulated than her mind. He, however, was far more interesting than anything that lay on the page. He was real, close and wet. His long-line shorts clung to him in all the right places, and they sat low enough on his hips to show off that magic v. She reached into her tote bag for the folded fan she always carried with her. Wishing they were in a private villa or a secluded island, she waved the fan at her face, trying to cool the flush that had crept up her cheeks. At least no one could see the response other parts of her body were having. He made it safely to the shore, and she watched his approach, willing him to look her way. All it would take was a smile, and she'd be dragging him inside to her suite. When his eyes finally locked onto hers...

Doorbell Rings

Dammit! Just when it was about to get good. I sigh, frustrated at the sudden interruption. Standing up from my desk, I take in the view from my office space located off the open living area. The space was supposed to be a breakfast nook, but I couldn't pass up the opportunity to write with that backdrop every day. Aside from the relative seclusion, it was the reason I bought the house in the first place a year ago. The forest beyond the pool provides plenty of inspiration for fantasy novels, and the crystal blue reflection in the water feeds the romantic in me. In fact, the scene that had just been interrupted began on the chaise nearest the French doors not 20 steps from the desk.

Mrs. Gingham? A voice calls from the other side of the mahogany front door. It is followed by a series of knocks.

"Yes, I'm coming." Why did they not just go away when I didn't answer the doorbell? If I were still in the city, they would have left by now. Hell, they might not have rung at all, just dropped whatever they came to deliver and left.

"Hello," I say with a feigned smile at the young man standing on the porch. He has just set the packages on the welcome mat and is rising from his squatted position when I open the door. His gray eyes sparkle when he looks up at me, taking in the fact I have on nothing more than a thin nightgown covered in a silk robe that hangs loosely on my shoulders and some fluffy slippers. Oops. If I were the character I had just been writing, I'd have pulled him inside the house, but I'm not, so I pull the robe closed. He keeps his eyes on me and smiles, showing the most beautiful white teeth I've seen in years. His head is shaved bald, but his chin is adorned with a glorious auburn beard that tames the cherubin roundness of his face. The occasional wiry grays poking through make me rethink his age.

"Good morning, ma'am," he says with just the hint of a drawl, like he is working to lose it but reverts to his natural accent when caught off guard. "I'm sorry to have interrupted your morning. Whenever I come to deliver to these remote parts, I like to check on people. It's easy for something to happen out here and no one know for days or even weeks."

A shudder runs up my spine. "You know, that sounds like something a serial killer might say," I respond, trying to hold in my smile.

Obviously startled by my joke, he begins stammering over his words. "No ma'am, I'm just trying to look out for our neighbors."

I laugh then, and he looks hurt for a moment before he, too, laughs. "Sorry. I'm an author, and everything is a story of sorts, even true crime stories."

"Oh, that would explain why we've gotten so many small package deliveries for up here recently. Are they your books?"

"No. Whatever time I don't spend writing, I spend reading. I am what many might call a book dragon. I read a lot, but I buy even more than I can read just in case I run out."

He smiles and bends down to retrieve the packages and hands them to me. My robe gapes open when I grab them, and his eyes once again take in the view before he catches himself and turns to leave.

"It was nice to meet you, Mrs. Gingham."

"It's Ms., and it was likewise a pleasure...um" I trail off realizing he hadn't introduced himself.

He turns back, showing those beautiful teeth again and responds. "The name is Asher."

And with that, he walks back to the mail truck he'd left running in the driveway. I watch him go. The uniform shorts hold snug to a wonderfully full ass. He obviously carries a few pounds in his midsection, but he is solid, like maybe he played football in high school, possibly college with the way his drawl is disappearing, and yet he enjoys a good meal. He has nice calves and broad shoulders. I shake my head at myself. With the way I am taking him in, one would think I hadn't seen a man in forever when, in fact, I had just left one on the page mere minutes ago.

He drives off with a wave out the window, and I go back into the house with the packages still clutched to my chest.

I spend the rest of the morning trying to get back into the head of my main character. Rather than seeing the hot surfer, though, my mind conjures a bald ginger with beautiful teeth. What in the world is wrong with me?

I finally give up and decide to take a dip in the pool before diving into one of my new books. I am really looking forward to the new mystery novel I'd heard about on social media. I chuckle aloud. So many people would say that I am too old to be spending time on those apps, but I find out about so many great books that way. I haven't yet begun to advertise my own works because I'm shy. Also, lots of people have said that social media works better if authors stick to one genre. I cannot focus on just one thing at a time. Hence, the romance I was writing this morning and the mystery I will likely spend the rest of the day reading. At some point, I should probably eat something too.

CHAPTER 2
KASSANDRA

I t takes two days before I can immerse myself back in my story. It takes less time for my audacious female main character to seduce the older hottie. She has no qualms about approaching men, though she prefers they pursue her, and she doesn't get ruffled when one shows up at her door.

***

Shar, still dressed in her white string bikini with coverup hanging off her shoulders, opened the door to her suite. She took in the surfer from the top of his head covered in wavy blond hair down to his bare feet. He obviously didn't waste any time on his attire before coming to meet her.

"Hey," he said in that carefree way only a beach bum could do. She let him drink in the view of her tanned skin that shone thanks to the oil-based lotion she'd used just moments before he knocked. She considered changing, but there was no use in being subtle. The appreciation in his eyes agreed with her assessment.

"Hi, yourself," she responded. "Would you like to come in?"

"I'm not dressed to go anywhere else, and my plan is for you to not be dressed at all."

She smirked, and stood in the open doorway, letting her coverup drop to the floor. He leaned against the jamb with his arm up, not bothering to close the door yet. She lifted her long blonde tresses from her neck and pulled the tie of her top loose. Holding those strings in the hand still holding her hair, she reached around her back with the other arm and pulled that tie loose as well. He raised a brow, and in one fluid motion, she released her hair and the top, letting both fall.

His eyes raked over her tits, and her nipples puckered under his scrutiny. His eyes had grown dark, and she shivered in anticipation. He wasn't as innocent as he looked. In fact, he was older than she had originally assessed, and she was glad she had read him right. She had no desire to play teacher today. Today, well, she would see what he could teach her. She grabbed the tie at her right hip, ready to bare it all, but he stayed her hand with a shake of his head.

"No, leave those. I'll take care of them later."

Heat pooled at her center, and she knew those bottoms were already damp. He pushed off the door frame and stalked toward her, pushing the door closed with his foot. He kept his eyes trained on hers as he walked her backward toward the seating area without touching her. Her breaths came faster.

"Lay on the couch," he said with an air of authority.

"Yes, sir."

He sat on the armchair facing her. "Touch yourself."

"Excuse me?"

"You heard me. Touch yourself. You've been thirsting over me since I first hit the sand this morning, so I know you're ready. Show me."

"And what will I get in return?"

He shook his head, eyes going hard, but he said nothing. Instead, he rose from the chair and walked toward the door.

"Wait, where are you going?"

She didn't want him to leave. She didn't even want to question him, not really. She just wanted him to touch her. That's what she thought they were here for. He seemed to be on the same page until the moment he sat in the chair. When he didn't stop, she stood and ran to get in front of him before he could open the door.

"Look, I'm not sure what just happened, but you caught me off guard. I thought you were going to touch me, that we would touch each other." She reached out a hand toward his chest.

He looked down at her, and what she saw in his eyes caused her to gasp, but she didn't move fast enough before his hand went around her neck, and he held her against the door. She stared at him wide-eyed and panting. No one had ever manhandled her like this before. Tears welled in the corners of her eyes at the pressure on her throat.

His voice was low, and his words came out more like a snarl. "I'm not here to do your bidding, little girl, nor am I here to be questioned. If you listen, we can both get what we want." Her vagina pulsed, and her eyes widened more, as if that were possible. Could she possibly be turned on by this? She didn't like domineering men...until him. "Are you ready to listen now, pretty?" Without a second thought, she nodded, at least as much as she could with his hand still pinning her to the door by the throat. He reached up with his free hand and wiped the moisture from her eyes. "I believe you. Now, go do as I said." She...

Doorbell rings

"She got up and answered the door," I say aloud, perturbed at the interruption just when the story was flowing nicely, just when they were getting to the good part.

"You have another set of packages, Ms. Gingham," says a familiar voice from the other side of the front door. I smile, thinking of the handsome young man and his auburn beard. His might have been the face of my next male main character if he would stop showing up at the most inopportune times.

I open the door. "Good morning, Asher." This time, I am dressed in lounge pants that fit snug across my hips, showing off my pudgy midsection, and a loose tee I have tucked into the front waistband to keep it out of my way. His gaze still takes me in from head to toe, sending a shiver down my spine. I am not starving for attention; I scold myself silently.

"You doing alright this morning?" he asks with a concerned look on his face. "You seem a bit flustered, and your face is flushed."

"Oh," I say with a bit of a laugh, "Yeah, I'm fine. I get my best writing done in the morning, and I was in the middle of an intense scene when you rang the doorbell."

He looks intrigued, like he is hoping I'll go into more detail, but I surely will not tell him that my male main character has just had the female main character by the throat, making her pussy wet before telling her to get on the couch and masturbate in front of him.

"Oh really? Well, I apologize for the interruption. Would afternoons be better for deliveries then? I could delay it a couple hours."

I am so shocked at his offer, 'That's a thing?' flies out of my mouth before I can stop it. "I mean, that's something you can do, just change your schedule like that?" I ask, trying to cover up my embarrassment.

He simply laughs. "It's a small town, ma'am. It's not like we have a ton of busy times we can't cover. It can get pretty boring somedays, which is why I come out to make deliveries." He looks past me into the house. The open door gives him a clear view of my desk across the large seating area.

I hope he isn't waiting for me to invite him in. I want to invite him in. I want to be as bold as Shar, but I'm not.

"Well, I don't want to inconvenience you from doing your job," I say to redirect the awkward turn this conversation is taking in my mind. "But yes, afternoons would be much better. Sometimes I can't get myself back on track for a day or two after an interruption."

"Oh no, I'm sorry. I hope that wasn't the case when I came the other day," he says, and I feel guilty for even saying anything.

I don't want him to feel bad. He had no way of knowing. He looks genuinely contrite, and I don't want his guilt. I want to reach out and touch his face. Stop it, Kass, you're not the main character of a book, I chide myself, sadness taking over my features, as the words fly through my mind in someone else's voice. I haven't heard from Charles in over a year, and definitely not since I left Mission City. Yet, his words still haunt me. He knew exactly what to say to hurt me, to make me feel less than, to put me back in my place.

"No need to apologize," I say quietly, trying to smooth things over but feeling a bit raw.

He must have noticed the change in my demeanor because his eyes take on that sincere concerned look again. It is the same one he gave me the other day that made my stomach flip flop. He is a big man, but when he looks at me like that, he makes me feel safe and warm.

"I'm sorry, I need to get back to work," I manage to eke out without my voice cracking or me falling into his arms. I head into the house.

"Ms. Gingham, your packages?"

"Oh." I turn back to him, willing the tears to hold off a few seconds longer. "Thank you for bringing them." I quickly grab the small boxes and mailers and retreat into the house, unceremoniously dropping them on the table next to the door.

"What in the hell is wrong with you," I say aloud. Almost too loud, I think when I realize he hasn't yet left the driveway. I sneak back to the door and look through the peep hole only to find him still standing there on the porch, his brows knitted above those beautiful gray eyes. I turn away and lean against the door willing him to leave. I need to work through this alone, and his presence is quite distracting.

I don't know how long we both stand in place before his footsteps mark him leaving the porch and walking up the gravel. I take a deep breath and blow it out slowly. A quick glance at my desk elicits a heavy sigh. I know there is no way I will get any more writing done today. Charles has ruined that. Maybe one day, he will no longer be my internal voice, but today is not that day.

CHAPTER 3
ASHER

I stand there staring at the door for what might have been an awkwardly long time if she had been watching. Her shifts in emotion are something I have never seen before, but they leave me bereft as soon as the door closes. She looked like she needed a hug but that she was afraid of being hugged. The tears in her beautiful hazel eyes were almost more than I could take. If not for the packages, I might have taken her into my arms and tested whether it was the hug she was afraid of or if it was something else. Shit, I need to get off the porch before she catches me standing here like a crazy man.

***

I walk back in the office and find Louise chatting with the town historian, and by historian, I mean gossip. She knows everything about everyone, and what she doesn't know, she makes up until she learns otherwise. I've known her my whole life, and I've tried to stay as far away from her as possible. Considering she's nearly my grandmother's age, you'd think she'd have learned to mind her business, but no, she's just as nosy now as she was when I was a kid. In fact, she is one of the reasons my childhood sweetheart and I never worked out.

Gabby, an apt name for the woman, told Carolyn that I had been in the news holding hands with another girl while I was off at college. It was a damn picture of me helping the Homecoming Queen up onto the platform because I was an underclass usher. Carolyn sent me a Dear Ash text. She wouldn't even hear the real story. By the time I got home, it was too late. Carolyn had already run off with this guy from out of town, and she was three months pregnant. Though that was years ago now, I still can't stand the ol' biddy.

"Mornin' Gabby," I say through clenched teeth. "Anything new happen while I was makin' deliveries?" I direct the question and all my attention to Louise.

"Now you know damn well ain't nothing happening in this town," Louise retorts. Gabby gives her a look, and she quickly adds, "except maybe that new person living out there in that big, secluded house down on Hampshed." Louise gives me a pointed look, cutting her eyes toward Gabby.

I shake my head at them both. I am not about to give them any details about Ms. Gingham. Though I know her first name because of her mail, I can't bring myself to call her anything more than what she has let me know was ok. I walk to the back ignoring the implied question. When I return, the question goes from implied to explicit.

"Have you met her? Seen her?" Gabby's eyes are locked on me, as if she is expecting some silent verification. Her lust for information on everyone turns my stomach, and I look for another reason to leave. If only I had waited a little while longer to make my deliveries or to return.

"Is she truly a recluse?" Louise's surprise-laced question catches me off guard.

Kassandra Gingham doesn't seem like a recluse. I mean, she answers the door easily enough for me. Though she always seems preoccupied, she isn't rude or hiding behind the door, like I imagine a recluse to do. She is just doing her author thing, which I assume keeps her busy. That thought reminds me that at some point, I need to grab one of her books. Maybe it will be a good conversation starter.

"No one in town has seen her since the moving truck left almost a year ago. It's like she took up residence but never leaves. She has her groceries delivered for heaven's sake. Who does that?" Gabby is damn near apoplectic.

"Lots of people in the city do that. It saves them time and having to deal with random people minding their business." I may have said that last part with a little more venom than necessary, but I want Gabby to leave. Thankfully, she takes the hint. With a look of disgust, she storms out the door, and I breathe a sigh of relief.

"That wasn't nice," Louise chides, though there is no heat in her words. She knows how I feel about Gabby.

"How do you put up with her?"

"Keep your friends close..."

"And your enemies closer," I finish. "Yeah, I get it, but I cannot abide that woman. I'm not going to contribute to her meddling in someone else's life, especially someone naive to Ms. Gabby Brewster." Louise laughs, and we both settle into the quiet pace of our closing routine.

"So, you have met her," Louise says quietly, as she walks into the back room. I smile. She won't pry, and I am grateful.

CHAPTER 4
KASSANDRA

The next morning, I am still struggling to clear my head. It has been a minute since Charles has taken over my thoughts and set my anxiety and imposter syndrome into overdrive. He and I have been estranged for over two years, and his voice had been silent since long before I came here to the Walsham River Basin. I don't know what brought it on yesterday, but I damn sure wish he would shut up again. I need to get back into Shar's head and that steamy scene Asher interrupted. I stand at the kitchen counter and look out beyond my desk with my cup of morning tea in hand.

The thought of Asher sends a shiver up my spine. He is so sweet and definitely attractive, but he is so young, so much younger than the men I am normally attracted to. He can't be more than 32, probably younger, and at 45, I feel like a cougar even thinking about his looks. That's why I have continued dating men older than me. It's a pattern I established in my early twenties, and it feels right. Older men help make decisions and ensure things are taken care of when I am overwhelmed or uncertain.

At least that's what I've always told myself, though it hasn't ever happened that way in my life. In my experience, they make decisions and expect you to follow through with those decisions without question. They drive the ship. It's exhausting and one of the reasons why all my female characters are strong, independent, and take the lead in their lives and relationships. I can't be like them, but I can create them and live vicariously through them.

Maybe it is the fact that Shar is thrown off-kilter by her current love interest that has my own thoughts going sideways. If Shar, who is always in control of her sexual escapades can be driven to submit, then who am I to think I can ever step outside of my comfort zone to grab the reins. Nah, it is just easier to stay to myself and keep my distance from men, even cute gingers who look like they give the best smothering hugs. It's better not to wonder if his beard is soft and whether it will scratch against the tender skin of my inner thighs.

As heat begins to rise at my thoughts, I feel the urge to finish the scene. In ten short steps, I am at my desk opening the manuscript I had slammed closed yesterday after Asher pulled off down the gravel driveway.

The surfer rubbed his beard while he watched her. His eyes had softened slightly from the slate rocks they had become when he got aggravated with her and threatened to walk away. They now had an intensity that turned her insides to jelly. That look promised a night to remember if she simply complied with his desires. Submission had never been one of her strong points, though, she'd never before met anyone who demanded it of her in such a way that had her pussy dripping. His eyebrows rose, and she realized she had stopped her manual manipulations.

Taking one of her fingers into her mouth, she wet it slightly and then rubbed that moisture into her nipples before she pulled and twisted them. Her legs bent up of their own volition, as more heat pooled between them. There was something immensely sensual about putting on a show for him.

"I'm waiting." His voice was deep and gravely, and she had to squeeze her legs together to relieve some of the tightness that traveled through her vagina. "Don't close up on me now. Show me what you wish my hands were doing. I know you're not innocent, so let's not play coy."

Shar locked eyes with him and slid her left hand into her bikini bottoms, her right hand continuing to squeeze her nipples, first one and then the other. When her fingertips grazed across her clit, a soft moan escaped her lips. She had already been hot for him when he arrived, and after his dominance at the door, the cloth barely covering her engorged sex was soaked. She wouldn't last for long with him watching, but she didn't want to stop. The heat from his eyes on her movements was such a heady turn on. She rubbed her clit in soft circles, increasing the pressure as the desire to close her legs grew.

"Mmmmm that's it. I can see you're finally settling in. Finger yourself."

She tensed. She was equally tired of him telling her what to do if he wasn't going to join her, and at the same time her pussy pulsed with each of his commands. She was left confused about how to respond, so she chose the side of pleasure and slid her other hand down from her breasts until she could plunge two fingers into her dripping slit. She pulled her left hand up to her mouth and sucked the taste of her own juices from her fingers, keeping her eyes on him. She moaned again, her arousal growing with each flick of her wrist. For a second, she was so overcome with the sensation that she closed her eyes and threw her head back onto the pillow.

He was standing in front of her with this cock out when she opened her eyes.

"Is this what you want, pretty?" She went to pull her hands

from her bottoms, and he shook his head. "I didn't tell you to stop. I asked a question."

Her body would not have listened to her mind at this point had she tried to control it. She was too far gone and too horny to not get that cock slammed inside of her. "Yes."

He smiled and knelt in front of her face. She smiled, as her hands went back to work on her pussy, and she opened her mouth to welcome him in.

Doorbell rings

⁙❖⁙❖⁙

"Fuck!" The word slips out of my mouth like a water cannon shooting through the silent house.

"Sorry to disturb you, Ms. Gingham. I waited until the afternoon."

I pull myself together, loosening my t-shirt from my taut nipples and rearranging my shorts to make sure it isn't clear just what he has disturbed me doing. I know the dampness will be visible if he looks closely enough. I am going to have to order a Do Not Disturb sign and hang it on the front door for whenever I am writing. I hold the knob for a full minute, calming my breaths before I finally pull the door open.

CHAPTER 5
ASHER

I've heard a lot of things through people's doors since I started delivering the local post, but I have never heard such a frustrated expletive as what comes from Kassandra. Ms. Gingham, I correct myself, lest I forget and accidentally call her by her given name. I don't think that will go over well, especially when my timing just seems to be getting worse. There is no real reason for me to knock on her door every day just to deliver one or two packages, but something makes me want to check on her, make sure she's okay. She looked so lost when she practically ran inside yesterday. It takes her so long to come to the door today that I decide to set the packages on the porch and leave.

She opens the door and steps directly in front of me before I can lay the packages down, and my breath catches. She smells like spring rain with hints of lavender, and her thick thighs are displayed beautifully in lounge shorts that hug them just right. It is all I can do to look straight up into her face rather than slowly take her in inch-by-inch. I don't even know this woman, and she is more irritated with me every day. What in the hell is wrong with me?

"Good afternoon, Asher," she says in a voice that matches

neither the frustration I heard moments ago nor the smile she has plastered across her face now.

"I'm so sorry. I seem to have interrupted you again. You said afternoon, so I thought it was late enough. Next time, I'll just leave the packages unless it's something heavy you might need help with." I know I am rambling, but I can't help myself. Something about her reels me in, and when she visibly relaxes into a genuine smile, I am at her command.

"It's alright, really. I did say afternoon. I just struggled to get started this morning, but that was not your fault, and you had no way of knowing. I do appreciate the personal delivery attention. Makes an old lady feel special."

I choke on my own spit. "Old? Ma'am, you are not old."

"Age is relative, young Asher. You call me ma'am, and yet I would not automatically call you sir unless…"

She cuts herself off mid-sentence and turns away from me. I take the moment to readjust my shorts. This was not a conversation I should be having during work hours with a client, and she is very much a client at this moment. Instead, I try to change the subject.

"Were you in the middle of another intense scene?" When she turns back toward me, her cheeks are red, and she pulls her shirt away from her body. If I wasn't so damn attuned to her, I wouldn't have noticed that her nipples are hard, and I wish I hadn't noticed. Dammit, I need to get out of here.

"What? Oh. Yes. The same scene actually. Well, a little further into it. But yes, it was…is…intense. I don't think I'll have a problem getting back into it today though."

"Oh, that's good. I was worried that I had ruined your whole writing mood."

When she looks up at me, her eyes darken, and I have the urge to readjust myself again. "No, you definitely haven't ruined the mood."

I peer into the house and toward the desk with its

beautiful view outside behind a laptop and two monitors. "Looks like a wonderful view to write in front of."

"Mhmm." She is looking at me with her eyes cloaked behind long, dark lashes. They are obviously natural, as she isn't wearing any makeup, and she doesn't seem the type to put on artificial ones to lounge around the house. "Lots of inspiration. I may switch it around one day, though, and try the front porch."

"Ma'am?"

"Oh, simply saying that the front porch affords an inspirational view as well. I just have never spent as much time out here."

I laugh. I'm not completely sure, but I have a feeling she has never stepped out on her porch for any length of time before. "Maybe one day I'll catch you out here, and that way I won't catch you off guard. You'll see me coming."

I nearly choke again at the words she mumbles. It sounds like she says she'd love to see me coming, and I'm not sure what to do with that. I mean, I know what my body wants to do with that, but damn, I need this job.

"Ms. Gingham?" I can't help myself. I want her to repeat what she'd said.

"Asher?" She smiles up at me. "I thought we had already introduced ourselves, you with your first name, and me with my last. Though, I'm sure you already know my first as often as you've now delivered my packages."

Delivering packages is the last thing on my mind unless it is my package she wants because it is screaming at me so loudly, I can't keep my mind straight. "Yes," I nearly growl out between heavy breaths. She takes a step back and leans against the door frame, her eyes wide. This isn't the fearfully uncertain look from yesterday. This look is something more, and if she has me follow her into the house, I'll make sure all uncertainty leaves her eyes. "Kassandra." She gasps, and my cock twitches. "My last name is McNeil," I say quietly and hold out my hand to her, as if we are meeting for the first time.

She looks down and then back up into my eyes. I'm not sure whether she is looking at my hand or elsewhere. God, please let her have been looking at my hand and not the throbbing bulge in my shorts. The thought no sooner enters my mind than she grabs my hand in hers, and my entire body goes stiff. Her hands aren't dainty and frail. They are strong and warm. They are the hands of a grown woman who has learned to give a firm handshake to ward off anyone who thinks her weak.

"It's a pleasure to meet you, ma'am," I say in the most hospitable manner I can manage considering my out-of-control libido.

"Likewise, Mr. McNeil. I would invite you in, but I am sure you have additional deliveries to make."

Deliveries? My brain glitches for a second. Oh, work. Yes, I am still on the clock and have more deliveries to make. "Yes, Kassandra. I do need to get back to work. Maybe next time I'll come closer to the end of the day." If I wasn't still holding her hand, I might have missed the shudder that runs through her. She smiles, and I berate myself for coming so early in the afternoon when I give her hand a small squeeze and let it go.

"I'll make sure I'm dressed a little more hospitably for company then."

The strength that it takes not to tell her how perfectly dressed she has been each time I've seen her is incredible. In fact, I want to tell her I'd like to see her undressed, but my brain takes over and leads me down the steps. I wave over my shoulder and step into the mail truck. "I'll see you soon, Ms. Gingham," I whisper to the truck's interior and make my way down the drive, sighing in relief when the uncomfortable tightness in my shorts relaxes once I get out of eyesight.

CHAPTER 6

KASSANDRA

When Asher drives away, I want to kick myself for suggesting he needed to leave. I sure as hell didn't want him to leave. The ache between my thighs certainly didn't want him to leave. Dammit, and me having not ordered anything recently. As I enter back in the house, I have the strange desire to order one item every day for the next month. But first, I need a moment back in my story to work out this thrumming in my vagina.

Of course, nothing this week seems to be working in my favor because as soon as I sit at my desk, my phone rings. I see my sister's name come across the screen, and I groan. I love her, but I don't feel like talking. She, on the other hand insists we talk every other day. Not only does she want to give me all the details of our hometown, a place I raced out of twenty years ago, but also people I have gladly forgotten about. She, however, cannot understand my reluctance to reminisce and gossip. Then she shares that she also heard from Charles, and I slouch in my chair. Though she does not live in the city, our town is close enough that she can keep tabs on everyone I knew there too. I really wish she wouldn't, though, because, once again, Charles' voice is sitting at the edge of my consciousness waiting for an excuse to lash out.

"Ok, and?" I try to fill those two words with as much sarcasm as possible.

"What do you mean 'and,' Kass? I'm telling you that he caught me out shopping yesterday and asked about you. I tried to avoid the conversation because I know how you feel about him, but damn, sis, you two were together for so long. He was like family."

"Toxic family, Malissa, remember? He damn near sent me into a nervous breakdown. He had me second guessing everything about myself, including my value as a woman." Tapping on the speaker phone icon, I get up and begin pacing in front of the windows that provides my beautiful view. I finally moved here, so I could get away from everyone who had known us as a couple. Why is it so hard for her to understand?

"I know. I'm sorry. He's just so stinking cute, even if he is nearly 20 years older than me, and he looked genuinely sad that he hadn't heard from you.

"Wait, you didn't tell him where I'm living now, did you? Lissa, please tell me you didn't even give him an inkling of where I am."

"No, I didn't. Hell, I don't even know where you are, not really. You've not invited any of us to come see you or the new house. Did you want to be a hermit?"

I laugh then. I really haven't been trying to isolate myself. I've simply been trying to find myself again. I wanted to get out a few more books, which is easiest to do in a quiet sanctuary, and I had to work through exorcising that menacing voice from my mind. Until the other day, I thought I had been successful.

"No, I'm not trying to isolate myself from you all. I just needed some time alone. Would you like to come out this weekend?"

"This weekend? How close are you?"

Again, laughter bubbles up from inside at my sister's response. I had been an only child for ten years when she was born, and then it was just the two of us in the house with our parents. No matter what I was dealing with, she always had a way of making me laugh, usually it was in response to how shocked she became at every little thing I said or did. At least, that's the way it was until I broke things off with Charles just months before our wedding.

"I'm close enough to drive out to get you mid-morning Saturday and make it back here before dinner. You're going to drive yourself, of course, because I'm not doing that, but it's possible."

"Holy shit, mom's gonna flip when she finds out that she could have brought you cookies multiple times."

Our mother's love, stress, and frustration languages are all cookies. We always bear the benefit, and the brunt, of her moods. I smile, rubbing my hands over my curves and squishy bits.

"You can bring some of those with you. But when I send you the address, please do not share it with anyone, including our parents. I'm not yet ready for them to just show up on my doorstep with a million questions."

"Right, so I'll just bring all of their questions with me," she says with a laugh. "I'm so excited and glad I have off this weekend. I've missed you."

"I've missed you too. Now, I need to get back to work. I have a deadline, and I'm falling further behind." I pull out my chair and plop into it, touching the mouse pad of my laptop to bring it back to life.

"Okay. I'll see you Friday night. Hopefully, there are some fun things to do around there." She disconnects the call before I can groan audibly.

I had hoped she would have gotten my hint about coming Saturday, but I should have known better. My sister is the take a mile each inch and maybe drag it out another 100 yards or so kind of person. I can't wait to see her. Her early arrival just means that I need to get this story out faster. I say a little prayer to the writing gods and try to fall back into my earlier scene.

⚜ ⚜ ⚜

The sky has gone dark by the time I finish that chapter. I grab a quick dinner of cheese, crackers, and grapes. It is not fancy nor protein-rich, but it is filling. I have a date with my shower and BOB. At the end of every spicy scene, I have always needed my own release. It's what has allowed me to move into the next parts of the story and maintain the plot without just writing pure erotica. Now, I love to read erotica, but my brain needs the stimulation of a plot, regardless of what my wayward body says. So, I carry myself upstairs and into the shower.

Feeling like a new woman, and not the frumpy aging author who lives vicariously through her characters, I climb into the bed and grab the package I'd dropped on the nightstand when I first entered the room. As I pull the tab to open the shipping package, my mind conjures Asher. What would he have thought had he known that this package wasn't a book? How would he have responded to knowing that he delivered my new inspiration? Would he have turned red? Been shocked? Offered to use it on me?

Those thoughts have my nipples puckering before I can even get the toy out of the packaging. It is not going to take long to finish tonight. I hold the small device in my hand looking for the on button. Thankfully, it is USB rechargeable and not battery operated because it already has a bit of a charge to it. It is the size of a large makeup brush, or one of those brushes they use after filing the acrylic at the nail salon, but instead of having a brush on the end, it has a round purple ball that begins pulsating as soon as I flip the switch. Yep, this will take no time at all.

I think about Shar and how well she had taken everything the surfer gave to her. His cock had filled her mouth completely and made her gag more than once. Between her fingers working on and in her throbbing sex, she had come near immediately when he began fucking her face without remorse. Though I've never had that experience myself, the thought of it has my pussy dripping. Everyone I've ever been with has treated me like an innocent, and I can never get them to see me as something more, as someone who wants more. I want to be desired and taken. I want to be taken by someone who legitimately wants me sexually and emotionally. I want to be my own main character.

Tears sting my eyes at the thought, and it is all I can do to push them back. I quickly push the pulsing ball against my clit and pull to mind the first male face I can imagine. The laughing eyes, ginger beard, and beautiful smile bring me back to the moment. I breath in and close my eyes. I imagine a bald head between my thighs, face down, beard tickling my sensitive skin. I giggle and gasp as the first strong pulses make waves through my vagina. Giving myself over to the feeling, I release all my pent-up frustration and need, barely flipping the switch into the off position before I fall asleep. I'll wash that magical device in the morning.

CHAPTER 7
ASHER

"Why the hell have you been moping around here the past few days? What's wrong with you, Asher?"

"Nothing's wrong with me. I'm just doing my job."

"Dude, you look like a puppy who's lost his new toy."

"Shut up, Louise, else you'll start sounding like Gabby."

"It's a good thing she's not here yet, else she'd be speculating even more."

"I'm going to get some lunch," I say, making my way toward the glass door to escape this conversation. "Do you want anything from the diner?"

"Yeah, bring me a Dr. Pepper."

I don't bother to respond, simply step out into the parking lot and take in the sounds of our small town. While we don't have a lot of people who live in town or hang out downtown during the day, there are still multiple cars traveling on Main Street. The temperature is a perfect 82 degrees for mid-June, and I wish I had a pool. I live in my parents' house, which previously belonged to my grandparents. It isn't the type of house I had imagined living in as an adult, especially not while playing SEC football at college.

I imagined myself in a new house, overlooking the water somewhere. It was going to be big enough to hold parties for my friends and family and yet have all the amenities that made me want to stay home, like a pool, a pool table, and a movie room. My parents' house was free, though. When I blew out my ACL in my junior year and then pulled a groin in my senior year, my career was completely over. Since mom was already sick by then, I came home to help take care of her. I've not found a reason to leave, but damn if I don't still dream of a house that isn't drafty and that makes me feel welcome.

Rather than take the truck, I decide to walk the couple of blocks to the diner. I wave to Mr. Johnson and Mr. Carter who are playing checkers at a card table they always set up in the McDonald's parking lot. Sometimes, I like to go chat with them for a bit. There is something soothing about listening to old people tell stories. I never believe half of their tales, as they are always the star athlete, war hero, main character type, the alpha of the pack. Everyone can't be the star, even when they seem poised to make it, but I still love to listen. Not today, though. I'm not in the mood, so I walk on.

Louise is right. I'm not quite myself, and each day seems to get worse. I try to think of any possible reasons my week that had started off so great is turning to shit. Nothing bad has happened. I mean, I know exactly what is bothering me, but I am trying hard to pretend it is something, anything else. Unfortunately, a pair of hazel eyes framed with thick, wavy chestnut hair penetrates my thoughts, and I can't deny that it is the lack of excuse to make the trip up her long drive that is bothering me.

I step into the diner with a wish for more package arrivals in the forefront of my mind. I'm just worried about our neighbor up there alone, I tell myself, as I wait for my order. Lunch is never anything fancy, some kind of sandwich and chips, maybe fries, and a Coke. Had to be Coke, not Pepsi, and definitely not some other abomination of a 'cola'. Coke was my grandpa's favorite drink, and it is one of the only vices I've kept over the years. If I would exchange even one of my daily Coke's for some water, like I used to in college, I'd probably be in better shape and not having my doctor make disappointed noises at me every time I deliver his mail. Or maybe I just need a new doctor and not the same one I've had since I was a kid. Fuck, this walk has not improved my mood any.

"Hey, sunshine," Gabby calls from her favorite stool to the side of Louise's counter.

"Who died?" I ask, ignoring her, as I walk through the locked door to hand Louise her drink and head to the back to eat my lunch.

"Hopefully not our friendly neighborhood recluse since she just got a large package today," Gabby responds with enough syrupy sweet sarcasm, I nearly gag.

"You actually have quite a few deliveries this afternoon," Louise calls back, not addressing Gabby's vulgarity. "Might be worth taking them in your truck, unless you want to come all the way back in town when you're done."

I turn away to hide the smile that spontaneously spreads across my face. I know exactly where my last delivery will be. Please let her be home and not in the middle of some intense scene when I get there. My faith isn't strong, but I figure it can't hurt to send up a request for some positive outcomes every once in a while.

"Cool, let me eat this sandwich, and then I'll get myself a route together."

◆◆◆◆◆

Gabby didn't lie about the size of the box clearly labeled with Kassandra's name on it. The return address is some publishing house in LA. Yes, jackpot. I keep meaning to buy one of her books, but I'm not sure if she writes using her own name or one of those pseudonyms. I'll never find her if she uses a pen name. Now, I can just bring up her books related to this box and possibly get a signed one from her directly.

I load the fifteen deliveries I need to make into the back of my Bronco, say my goodbyes to Louise, and Gabby, who is, unfortunately, still there. Stupid ass home training. Sorry, momma. She'd have hated me wishing ill about someone, even Gabby Brewster, but I have a real hard time not wanting to choke that woman, and not in a fun way. I climb into the truck, look down my list of addresses again, smile at the final one, and pull off down the road.

Normally, my afternoon deliveries, even for this many, only takes me about an hour or so, but my goal of making Kassandra the final stop has me traveling from one corner of town to the other and back again. It is late afternoon before I pull onto the gravel that leads to her house. The driveway itself is about 300 yards, keeping the house out of view until the last curve. Then it opens on a huge clearing with enough parking for at least 50 SUVs before anyone would need to touch the grass.

The house itself is beautiful, a deep forest green with wood accents that look perfect against the forest backdrop. There are at least two stories and an attic, or possibly three stories. It is hard to tell by just looking at the front. The porch spans over half of the facade and is deep enough for multiple swings and rocking chairs. She keeps the decoration simple with two chairs, a small table between them, and a large porch swing that lays flat like a bed. The landscaping is also simple but well kept. Having looked at and held her hand before, I have no doubt she pays someone to do that task.

I don't know why I'm procrastinating. I'm excited to see her again. These three days with no deliveries have ruined my whole week, and as I sit here, I suddenly get nervous. Has she been happy I haven't come to interrupt her work? What if her face falls as soon as she sees me? C'mon, Ash, get yourself together. She's just a nice lady who is new and interesting. If she were a local, you wouldn't be so worked up. I get out of the truck and grab the box.

CHAPTER 8
ASHER

She must have been watching through the window because I no sooner step onto the first stair when she opens the door looking just as beautiful as ever.

"Asher, how good to see you!" Her smile is so warm, I want to bask in it.

"I would have come back sooner, but you didn't have any packages come through."

"I know. Although it seems like I was having daily deliveries last week, I really don't order things all the time. That one looks heavy."

"I can put it inside for you if you'd like," I offer, trying to keep my eagerness from coming through. I'm not sure how I'll respond if she says no.

"That would be wonderful! I'm sure I could manage on my own, but I'd be remiss to turn down such a generous offer."

Is she flirting with me? I know our ages are quite different, and maybe women her age act differently from those my age, but I really hope she's flirting.

She holds the door open for me. "You can put it on the counter," she points toward the far end of the kitchen island near her desk area, "there by my office, so I can check them and put them away."

"Are these your books?"

A slight blush comes to her cheeks, but she turns away quickly and closes the door. "Yes, they are. It comes out soon, and I've already had a few orders I will need to fulfill on the release date."

"That's awesome!" I say, not hiding my enthusiasm. I love when people can do the thing they love and have success with it. "Can I see?"

"Really?"

"Yeah. It's not every day I get to meet a famous author. In case you haven't noticed, this is a pretty small town in the middle of nowhere."

She chuckles. "I may have gathered that when I drove in months ago. It's one of the reasons I've not felt the need to go anywhere."

"Wait, have you really not left the house since you moved in?"

Silence. She watches me, looking deep into my eyes, like she is searching for something. I'm not sure what she is trying to find, but I desperately hope she sees it there. It is nearly a full, uncomfortable, minute before she answers.

"I've been busy. That box you're still holding is my third book I've written this year."

"Holy shit! For real? I thought books took far longer to write and publish and all of that. That's amazing!"

She turns wide eyes on me, and I want to fall into their depths. I look away for fear I'll do something stupid like reach out to cup her cheek when I realize I really am still holding the box of books in my hands. I quickly turn toward the counter she had indicated and place the box on its surface. I see her move away from me in my peripheral vision and look up to find her walking around the counter on the other side. If I hadn't seen her, I wouldn't have known she'd moved. She moves so smoothly, her steps soft and sure, unlike me who sounds like I'm clomping through a barn in clogs whenever I walk across the floor.

She opens a drawer I can't see and turns toward me with a steak knife held blade up in her hand. Though, I'm not necessarily afraid of her, I instinctively take a step back and raise my hands in mock appeasement, making sure to keep the smile on my face. She stands looking at me for so long, I almost second guess my assessment of her, but then she giggles and slides the box over to her side of the counter, using the knife to cut through the tape.

"Very often it does take a while to get books published," she says, as she opens the flaps and pulls out a long strip of brown shipping paper. "I am what is considered a hybrid author. I have some books that go through a publisher, and those take up to a year to come out after I finish them. So, for example, this one..." She holds up a book with a purple cover ornately designed in gilded vines "was written early last year and submitted after editing in August. It will hit the shelves in a few weeks. It's a romantasy," she says, setting it on the counter and pushing it my way.

"Romantasy? So, romance and fantasy?" She nods with a huge grin. I can't help but be bolstered by her approval. I'm not some dumb jock, and I hope she doesn't think so. It is hard not to be intimidated by someone who is successful writing books, though, when sometimes I can't even think of the right words to say to her. Instead, I look down at the book. "Trials of the Meridien, huh?" I don't bother to look up at her. I can feel her watching me, and I need to compose my thoughts a little better. Instead, I walk over to the seating area and sit down to read the blurb on the back.

She doesn't move or say anything, just stands there. "This sounds good," I say, trying to cut the tension, or at least reduce how tense I am feeling. I flip the book over. "So, you don't write under your name then?" I hadn't meant to say that aloud, but now that it was out, I look toward her for some kind of response.

She eyes me warily with a look that says she's waiting for a punchline. "Well, you're holding a book I told you was mine, and the author's name doesn't match the one I told you was mine, so you draw the conclusions." She has both of her hands on the countertop, almost as if she is about to climb over it, but still, she doesn't move.

"No need to get feisty, ma'am. I simply meant that I had intended to go look for your book online, but I wasn't sure what name to look for." I barely finish the first sentence before the serious look on her face breaks, and she is in tears with laughter when I stop speaking. "What's so funny? The fact that I wanted to read your book?"

She holds up a hand and takes a couple of steadying breaths. "No. No. The look on your face when you said I was being feisty. It was priceless." She walks around the counter and sits across from me. "Thank you. I needed that laugh. It's been a week. I am glad you came by to bring my books and stopped in to chat. I sometimes forget how nice it is just to talk to someone besides my characters. Maybe I'll legitimately take a bit of a break when I finish this current book. I've not taken even a whole week off in a year. Thank goodness for movers, so I didn't have to stop working last year."

The flush in her cheeks makes the darker tones of her hazel eyes pop, and I am lost again. This woman is gorgeous without even trying. Now some might call me impulsive, but my next words have me even reconsidering my self-control ability. I can't let the moment go without at least trying, right? The worst she can say is no.

"What if you took a couple hours off now and joined me for dinner?"

There's that look again. The fawn before the flight. Shit, I should've stopped myself.

"Really?" She looks at me with her head turned toward the

side like she isn't sure she heard me correctly, but the uncertainty in her eyes tells the truth. Rather than draw attention to the underlying emotion, I choose to respond to the question.

"Sure, unless you've already had dinner."

She turns toward the kitchen, which is slowly being cast in shadows as the sun falls below the tree line at the back of the house. She hasn't yet turned on the interior lights, and we will both be in the dark soon because of the forest cover. She looks back at me biting her lip and shakes her head. "How much attention will it garner for me to walk into a restaurant in town after never having shown my face? Will we be the talk of town gossip tomorrow?"

"Is that what you're worried about? Is that why you've not left the house?"

She looks down and worries that lip again with her teeth. I need her to stop that, else I will be needing something else. She stands and starts to walk past me toward her desk. I grab her hand to keep her nearby.

"I'm sorry. You don't have to answer that question. It's none of my business, really, and I'm not trying to force you to show your face to the town if you don't want to. I just would really like to have dinner with you." I look up into her eyes and watch her relax some, enough that I think it safe to stand. "Do we have gossips here? We're a small town. Heck yeah, we have gossips. Truth be told, though, they've already been talking about you, about the fact that no one has seen you, about the fact that you have your groceries delivered. About..."

"Oh my god, my groceries!" She pulls her hand away and puts it to her chest. It is all I can do not to laugh at the gesture. "Do people not have their groceries delivered? That's the best damn thing to have come about in the past five years." She begins pacing back and forth in front of the counter. "I can't believe they talk about my groceries."

I can't hold it back any longer. A chuckle escapes, and she

stops in her tracks to glare at me. I laugh even harder. Fuck, she is beautiful riled up over nothing. "You know, you could teach them a lesson and show your face at the diner. I was going to suggest the somewhat less local restaurant out on the highway, but if you really want to see what life is like here, the diner is the place to go." Her glare falters, and a spark of mirth lifts her cheeks. Before a moment passed, she, too, is laughing aloud.

"I'm not ready for all that. I will try the highway restaurant first."

Smiling at my small win, I gesture graciously toward the door. "Shall we then?"

"Like this? I'm not going like this! In lounge pants and a tank top?" She puts her hand on my chest and pushes me back onto the chair. She then takes off running up the stairs, her ass bouncing with each lift. The skin beneath my shirt burns where she touched me, and my heart is trying to escape my chest, but I sit back, pick up the book and wait.

CHAPTER 9
KASSANDRA

Holy shit, am I really going out to dinner? Am I actually going to leave this house. Wait, did Asher just ask me out? Breathe, Kass, breathe. My hand still tingles where I had pushed him into the chair. The sparks had me wanting to jump onto his lap, so I opted to run up the stairs instead. Now, what the fuck am I going to wear? Geez, I've not put on real clothes in nearly a year.

I pull out a pair of black leggings that almost look like pants if no one looks closely and a top with a deep V neckline that hugs the girls well. I pair it with knee-high boots and a large tote. I love an oversized bag, even if it holds nothing in it. A quick glance in the mirror tells me everything looks okay up to my neck. But my god, what am I going to do with this hair of mine? It is thick and unruly on a good day, but I haven't even brushed it today, so this is not going to be easy.

Yanking the brush through my hair, I pile it on top of my head into a loose bun, letting a few tendrils fall around my face. I'm surprised Asher doesn't come running up to check on me when I yelp at a particularly large knot near my nape. Oh shit, how long have I been up here? Let me get going! A couple coats of mascara and some lip gloss finish the look, and

I make my way back down the stairs to find him relaxed in the recliner reading my book.

The way I stop in my tracks before my feet hit the floor. He is reading my book. I let him look at it, but I didn't expect him to be there reading it. Deep breaths.

"I'm ready if you are."

"One second, I'm almost done with this chapter."

Seriously? Stop reading! Please stop reading in front of me. Of course, I don't say any of those words because what kind of author asks a reader not to read their books. I just didn't think he would want to read it after I told him the genre.

"So, this is a romance, right? I'm guessing Kalli and Jordan will get together."

I nearly choke as I take the final steps onto the main floor. "No, absolutely not."

Holding the book in the air, his brows knit like he can't believe what I'm saying. "What do you mean? They seem great together."

I walk past him, grabbing the book on my way through. "You'll just have to read it and find out. I'm not going to give the story away." Taking a pen from my desk, I open the cover and sign the first page:

Asher,
I hope you love a good plot twist.
M. Knightsong

I can't believe I'm signing a copy of my book for him and almost daring him to read it. Maybe he'll just put it in his truck and forget it exists. I walk back and hand him the book saying, "Let's go. I'm hungry."

"Yes, ma'am," is all he says as he follows me out, pulling

the door closed behind him. This time, his drawl is thick, and I shudder at the sound of it.

He isn't kidding about the restaurant being on the outskirts of town. I don't recognize it because it is in the opposite direction from the way I arrived. But there it stands, lights everywhere, like it's a beacon in the darkness. Coming around the curve to find it almost reminds me of flying over the mountain into Vegas. Suddenly, the sky is lit, and you can't help but watch it come into view.

The large sign outside of the Country Tavern Steakhouse boasts live music on Fridays and daily happy hour drink specials. I'm not even sure what day it is, and I'm too embarrassed to ask Asher. If there is a live band, I'll know it's Friday, and if there isn't, I won't lose face.

When we get out of his Bronco, my nose is assaulted by the smell of farm pastures, dirty hay and cattle. Where in the hell have we driven to? I never smell that from my house, and we didn't drive but 20 minutes to get here. We round the corner of the restaurant, and my answer comes in the shape of a bull, a live bull, standing in a pen covered in hay.

"What in the world," I exclaim, not sure what else to say.

"What?" His tone intimates that this is all normal, everything here is normal. How in the world is this normal? Is it supposed to be ironic that a steakhouse has a live bull outside its doors? That doesn't seem funny ironic to me, more like awkward.

"Are they trying to tell us he might be our dinner?"

Asher laughs and shakes his head. I make to glare at him, but the door to the restaurant opens, and someone brings out a pail of what looks to be various weeds and grass, pouring it into the short trough sitting on the side of the pen.

"How are you doing, Brone?" The kid with the pail asks, lightly patting the bull on its neck. I have never seen a domesticated bull before. I didn't even know they could be domesticated. I look at Asher, and he gives me a noncommittal shrug, grabbing my arm and leading me through the door.

"That thing has a name and lets people pet it," I ask in a whisper as the door behind us closes.

"Yes. He has been the restaurant's mascot since it opened about 15 years ago. People come from all over to take pictures with Brone. There are pictures along the hallway leading to the restrooms from those that have shared their photos with the owners."

I can't think of anything more to say, so I start walking down the long entryway toward the hosts' desk. The place is super rustic with wood everywhere, as if it really were an old-timey tavern. A server passes in front of us, and all the glassware is mason jars. I know I have moved to a rural part of the state, but this is far beyond expectation.

"You said this restaurant had been here for 15 years now. Did they build it to look this way for the aesthetic?"

"Not exactly." He takes a couple steps to the right and then to the left, as if looking for someone, and then takes my arm again. "If I see the owner, I'll call him over to explain the history to you. I could tell you, but he spins a great tale that I think the storyteller in you would enjoy much more." He isn't wrong, as I was already thinking about how I can incorporate this place into one of my books.

"Hey there, Asher," the young hostess says, as we make our way to the desk. "So good to see you." She is super bubbly, maybe 25 years old, though her enthusiasm has me thinking she is a bit younger still. The doe eyes she makes at him gives away the motive behind her demeanor, but he seems oblivious to it.

"Hey. Can we get a table for two down near the front windows?"

"Um, sure. Give me a sec to get one cleaned off."

The place isn't overly busy, and since the only music I hear is clearly streamed in through a sound system, it isn't a Friday. Either they are short staffed, or she needs a moment to compose herself before seating us.

"Follow me," she says once she has grabbed a couple of menus and napkin-wrapped utensils. Her sweetness has dulled a bit, and she seems all business now. I can't help but feel sorry for her.

"She a friend of yours?" I ask nonchalantly, once we're alone at our table.

"Huh? Who? Oh, Sarah, no. She's a baby."

"I'm not sure she's a baby anymore, but she's definitely a fan."

"She's the baby sister of one of my best friends from high school. She was an unexpected addition to their family, as Jesse, my friend, had been the youngest for about ten years when she was born."

I bite my lip to not blurt out that brother's best friend is a very popular trope, especially with younger female readers. Nor do I mention the probable age gap between us. He seems completely uninterested in her or that conversation, so I don't want to make the night awkward. Then I realize his eyes are fixated on my lips and slowly release the skin, licking the spot once it springs back in place. He starts coughing and reaches for the glass our server has placed on our table.

"Are you okay?"

He holds up one finger and nods, taking a few more sips of the water. "Yeah, I'm good. You'd think that by this age I'd have mastered the art of breathing and swallowing at the same time."

Several heads turn in our direction at my laugh. On top of being attractive and super sweet, Asher is also witty. Either that, or I am definitely suffering from my unintentional isolation. I am going with the former.

"So, is this your hometown then?" He smiles, but there is something missing from the smile, something sad in his look reduces it. I almost think he isn't going to answer. "Sorry if that was a little forward. You just seem to know a lot about the place. That hostess is the sister of your high school best friend, and while something about you says you would fit in somewhere much more suburban, maybe even urban with time, you are comfortable here." He appears to process my explanation with some significant consideration before he answers.

"Yeah. I was born about 20 minutes from here at the only hospital in the county maybe a month after it was built, at least that's the story my parents told. I came back here after college because my mom was sick and living alone. Needless to say, even after she passed, I didn't leave."

The sadness that comes over his face triggers my guilt. Heaven knows I keep to myself enough that I know how to mind my business. "I'm so sorry. I didn't mean for you to relive difficult times."

"It's okay, really. It's been many years now. I just sometimes wonder what my life might've been if I hadn't come back here."

"Well, I can tell you that my past week would have been much less interesting." I hold my breath for a second waiting for his response. Thankfully, his chuckle bubbles up, and he looks into my eyes for the first time since he started answering my question. Then I get a glimpse of those beautiful teeth as his smile returns, and my stomach flutters. I am far too old for butterflies. He is far too young to give me butterflies, not that his age has stopped any of the thoughts I've had about him over the past week.

"Where are you from, then?" His question catches me off guard, though it probably shouldn't have, but I am grateful for the server who comes to take our order. She gives me a moment to think. Do I really want to share my life with him, and do I want to share it in such a public place?

"I grew up in a town about six and a half hours northwest of here, but I spent the better part of the last 15 years in Mission City."

"And you decided to move back to a small town?"

I smile at his incredulity. It makes sense that he wonders about my choices in the same way I wonder about his. Neither one of us fully embodies this small-town world, and yet, here we are.

"Asher, so good to see you, my friend," a friendly, older voice comes from a row of tables up from us. A tall, dark-skinned man maybe in his early 60s with a head full of tightly faded white hair walks toward our table, squeezing behind servers and making his way down between the levels. He reaches out and shakes Asher's hand.

"Hi Jerry. How's Jeanie?"

"She's been under the weather the past couple days. Hopefully, it's just a bug, but you know it's hard to talk that woman into seeing a doctor."

"Funny, she says the same about you." The two men laugh, and I'm left sitting there watching the exchange, not sure if I should say anything or not. Asher makes the decision for me. "Jerry, I'd like you to meet my friend Kassandra. She's relatively new here, so I'm just kinda showing her around."

"Nice to meet you, Kassandra. I hope you come back when my Jeanie is here. She's loves to meet the new people around the area and offer you free pie."

"That's very sweet. I hope I'll get to meet her soon. And please, call me Kass. Kassandra sounds so formal." I see Asher's eyes widen, and it takes all my control not to laugh at him. Instead, I decide to change the subject completely. "Ash tells me that there's an interesting story about the creation of this restaurant and the history of this building. I was so surprised to see Brone outside and was curious. He said I should hear the story directly from you." Asher again reacts in the most comical way possible to my shortening his name, and I snort into my napkin, playing it off for Jerry as if I had to sneeze.

"Oh man, that's such a great story. Asher, you bring her by early next week before we open, and we will tell you the story. It's much better told when Jeanie is here to make sure I don't miss anything."

His eyes get that distant look in them again, and my heart melts for the man who is missing his lady being by his side. One of the reasons I write romance is because I'm a sucker for a great love story. Of course, I've not experienced one, so mine aren't necessarily the sappy sweet kind, but I love those too, nonetheless. "That would be wonderful, and if Asher is too busy, I'd gladly come down for a drink and a story." Jerry smiles widely and then makes his way to the other tables, greeting each customer in turn.

"He's very nice, and it's obvious he misses Jeanie being here with him."

"Yeah, they're great people, and they're good for each other. Not all couples are good for each other."

I open my mouth to ask about that last statement and then close it again when our server comes with the ton of food we had ordered. This time my mouth opens in surprise at the sheer quantity. I am a big woman, and I love to eat, but there is no way I'll be able to finish all this food in one meal, even with help.

"It's a lot, I know. I just didn't know if you'd ever bring yourself out here again, so I wanted you to try a little of everything. Don't worry, you can wrap up whatever you want to go."

I grab a piece of a yeast roll and dip it in the honey butter. A moan escapes my lips as soon as it hits my tongue. This is so much better than anything I've made for myself this past year. It's not that I can't cook. It is simply that I hate cooking for and cleaning up after myself. The fun of cooking is in sharing the meals. At that thought, I smile at my companion and cut off a piece of steak from the plate sitting directly in front of him, making sure to get some of the fat too. The meat melts in my mouth like the buttered roll had.

"If you could capture that look of ecstasy in your book descriptions, every man would want to read it." Asher's gaze is glued to my face when I open my eyes, and I feel heat rise from my neck into my cheeks. "No, ma'am, no need to be embarrassed. I'm so glad you're enjoying the meal. Would you like another piece of steak?" He cuts off a piece of the fatty end with a question in his eyes, offering the fork in my direction. Does he want me to take the fork? Or does he want me to eat the meat from his fork? It isn't a large piece that I will need to put on my plate and cut into bite-size pieces. Before my insecurity can rise any higher, I lean forward, not taking my eyes off his, and take the steak into my mouth, closing my lips around the end of his fork.

It feels like the entire restaurant goes quiet, and it is just us in the room. He continues to stare at my mouth as I let the fork go to sit back and enjoy the morsel. His gray eyes have gone dark, and the look he gives has me clenching my thighs together against the pulsating response.

CHAPTER 10
ASHER

What in the world is happening? In one moment, I'm trying to distract her from the embarrassment of my ill-timed one-liner. In the next, she is staring into my eyes and putting her lips around my meat, or rather the piece of steak I'm holding out for her. What does that mean? Is it flirting? An invitation? Simply a misunderstanding of what I'm offering? My cock doesn't seem to care what the answer is. He is standing at attention imagining those lips wrapped around him. Ok, it is my brain with the imagination, but damn if my cock isn't riding along on that train wreck.

I close my eyes for a moment and looked away only to land on Gabby fucking Brewster. "Shit!" I don't mean to say that aloud. I don't want to ruin the moment happening between Kassandra and me. I just can't believe Gabby managed to find her way out here tonight. Then I see Sarah standing near her table and my blood boils. I forget that Gabby is their great aunt, and I bet that little brat called her. I wonder what she said. Did she tell her that I'm here with some random woman? Did Gabby have her watching for an unfamiliar woman to show up in town? Either way, I am not going to let them ruin Kassandra's first night out of the house.

"Is everything alright?" Kassandra asks, concern etched on her face.

I take a deep breath trying to figure out how to salvage our dinner, still enjoy the evening, and get her out of here unscathed. "Do you remember how I said that, of course, we have some major gossipers around here?" She nods, her brows still furrowed, obviously waiting for me to continue. "Well, the biggest one just got here." She starts to look around, but I stop her. "Don't make eye contact. She's like a bull, and eye contact is a red flag." She turns back to me, the corners of her mouth pulled up slightly, and I can't hold back my own laugh.

"That's a terrible analogy." She is trying so hard not to laugh out loud.

"Maybe so, but it's the truth." I grab her hand from the table and feel a hum of electricity run through my fingers at the touch of her skin. "Let's just continue to enjoy our dinner, and then I'd like to show you something out back here before we leave. We only need to make it another thirty minutes."

"Asher, I'm not afraid of gossip. That woman doesn't even know me."

"She's already caused enough damage in my life," I say, maybe a little too forcefully. Kassandra frowns but says nothing, putting a forkful of food in her mouth without really looking at it. "Sorry. That woman has a history of destroying relationships, and I do not want to be on the receiving end of her work again."

"I understand," is all she said before swallowing her bite. Then she puts her fork down and takes a sip of her wine. It is of the fruity white variety, but I am not a wine guy, so I have no clue what that even means. I assume it means the wine tastes like juice. The way her nose lifts at the end of her sip doesn't look like someone who has finished off a glass of juice, but maybe it is from the situation and not the drink itself. Suddenly, the night is not going the way I'd hoped.

"Hey. I'm sorry. I invited you out and now I've made a

mess of it for something that really has nothing to do with you."

She folds her hands together on the table and looks up at me. The previous openness of her gaze is no longer there, and I could kick myself. I let Gabby fuck this up, and she hasn't even said a word, hasn't even approached us. Better yet, I am fucking this up.

"We can go if that would make you more comfortable. When you talked about the gossipers earlier this evening, I thought you were worried about me. I hadn't even considered that you might have had your own issues with them. I don't want us to sit here if you are uncomfortable."

I quickly grab her hands. I can't think of anything else to do. She has this all wrong, and I don't know how to fix it, but I must fix it. I have to salvage the wonderful time we've been having. "I was worried about you and the response you would get if everyone realized you were the woman up in the big house. I, honestly, didn't expect to have any personal reaction at all, other than trying to make sure you were comfortable. I've messed up your night, and I hope you won't hold it against me."

I release one of her hands and wave for the server to bring us a couple of boxes. While we wait, I grab Kassandra's hands again and hold them. She looks down at our entwined fingers for a long while before lifting her eyes back to mine. There's confusion written in the scrunch of her nose and disappointment in her eyes, but I don't see anger. I breathe a sigh of relief and smile. She doesn't return my smile, but she also doesn't look away.

"You have a beautiful smile," she says after what feels like an awkwardly long silence. "I couldn't write a character with better teeth."

Heat rushes up my neck, and I close my eyes as my ears get hot. It's bad enough I'm a ginger, but it's horrible when I blush because my ears turn just as red as my beard. For the first time since my hair started falling out, I found myself wishing I had continued to let it grow, so it could cover the beacons now shining on both sides of my head.

She is smiling when I open my eyes again. I'd set my whole body on fire just to keep that smile on her face rather than the indescribable slew of negative emotions marring it just moments ago. Before I can say anything, the server brings our boxes and the check. I slip her my credit card without looking and help pack up the entire meal that was left on the table. It's not that we haven't eaten anything. We have. They simply pile on the food, making it a great value for the price.

"Here, let me pay the tip," Kassandra offers when the server brings back my card and receipt. I start to argue that I had invited her to dinner, but she quickly lays a twenty on the table and sets to putting our food boxes in a bag. I thank the server and start leading Kassandra toward the back door of the restaurant.

"Where are we going? This doesn't take us out toward the car."

"I told you I wanted to show you something outside."

Her half smile told me that she had forgotten that little detail, and I laugh quietly. I know she would never get a view like this from her house, even if her daily view was lovely. "C'mon, we're going to miss it if we don't hurry, or there will be a bunch of people in the way." I grab her hand and just about pull her through the door and down the short path to an open seating area with picnic benches and small fire pits.

"What is this?"

"This is where the staff comes to hang out during their breaks and when they have friends and family events. It is also the best place in the entire county to watch the sunset."

"Oh really? You're the expert on this then?" She raises an eyebrow at me, and I know it is bait, but I let myself get hooked.

"Yes, ma'am. I am always scoping out the most beautiful

views. If I stand just right, tonight, I'll get two at the same time."

Her mouth drops open and then quickly closes, her bottom lip slipping between her teeth. That right there is definitely one of the best things I've seen in years. When the sky erupts in beautiful shades of pinks and purples across the blue expanse, I put my hands on her shoulders and turn her around to see it. The gasp that explodes from her says I have proven myself right. I pull out my phone and take a silhouette photo of her in front of the backdrop. She'll want this memory, I tell myself.

"It's absolutely stunning!"

"Yes, it is," I respond with a whisper.

She reaches into her pocket and pulls out her phone to begin snapping photos of the sky. The sky alone would never compare to her standing in front of it, so I reach out a hand, silently asking for her phone. She looks at me funny for a few moments and then reluctantly hands it over.

"Turn your head to look back at me." She does so, and I snap a photo that takes my breath away. "Beautiful," I say, clicking the shutter button a few more times for good measure before handing the phone back.

"Thank you for this and the photos," she says, stepping closer and kissing my cheek. Once again, my breath catches, but then she asks something I never expected to hear. "Take a selfie with me? I want you in this memory too."

Without a word, I walk closer, turn my back to the sunset, and put my arm around her shoulders. She lifts the phone, so the screen is facing our direction and tries to get a good angle to include us both and the sunset. It is a struggle because there's nearly a foot difference in height. Finally, I take the phone from her hand and hold it out to get the full view. She beams into the camera, and I smile looking at her. *Click*

CHAPTER 11

KASSANDRA

The evening has been a rollercoaster. Lots of surprises, and some unexpected anxiety, but it ends on such a strong note that the ride home in silence feels stifling. What is he thinking? Is he still upset about the town gossip? Maybe he is still uncertain about all my personal questions? I wish I could read his mind like I can my characters'. No matter whose point of view I'm in, I always know what the other person is thinking. Not so with Asher.

I reach out and touch the hand that sits on top of the gear stick. "Thank you for a wonderful evening." I genuinely mean the words, but the way he looks at me, hardly looking at me, says that he doesn't quite believe them. I begin worrying my lip, pulling it between my teeth and biting the skin inside. Though I am an author, I sometimes struggle with finding the right words to say in stressful situations, and silent car rides are the worst. Whenever Charles was silent in the car, I knew an argument was coming once we got to the house. I remind myself that Asher is not Charles. Hell, we aren't a couple, nor do we live together. If he wants to start a fight, he can just drop me off and take himself home.

Instead, I feel his hand move under mine. He slowly flips

his hand over and laces his fingers between mine. Without a single word, he eases my mind, and I feel my heartbeat slowing to a normal rhythm. I look out of the window into the dark night and smile.

He turns onto my street, even without the benefit of sufficient lighting or signage. I don't think I could find my way that easily. In fact, I know I couldn't have, at least not without GPS, and I would have still likely missed the turn. "I hope you'll share that picture of us with me," he says, breaking the silence.

Pulling my phone from my pocket, I open the photos from tonight. There are so many more than I expected. I scroll through them finding the ones I like the most and click the share button. "What's your cell number?" Once I send them, I save his number into my contacts and chuckle to myself.

"What's so funny?"

"That was such a smooth way of asking for my phone number, and I just gave it to you without a second thought."

He snorts his laughter, and I see him shrug in the shadows. "You caught me," he says, mirth evident in his voice.

By the time we make it up my driveway, my heart is fluttering again. This time, it is from him rubbing his thumb across my fingers in a slow, steady pattern. He comes around the truck and helps me climb down. I don't remember the climb up being so high, but the dark does something to my depth perception, and I nearly fall out of the door into his arms. With an embarrassed giggle, I wrap my arm around his and let him walk me to the door.

"Oh shoot, the leftovers," I say, looking back at the truck.

I have never realized how little light there is in my front yard area until I strain to watch his ass as he runs back to the truck. That will be fixed this week. "I really need to get some lights put up out here," I muse when he returns with the bag of to-go containers. "You could have tripped over something and broken your neck."

"Oh, you were worried about me, were you?" The smirk on his face gives away his doubt.

"Of course. What else might I have been worried about? It's not like I've had anyone else out here at night to have noticed just how dark it gets."

After a short moment of staring into my eyes, he acquiesces and agrees that I probably should have some more lights put up. He also makes a good point that anyone could sneak up on me through the woods and I would never know it, so I should include some motion activated lights out front and back. I don't tell him that I do have some in the back, but I turn them off when I go out for late-night swims. Not that I expect anyone to be around looking, but I don't want any prying eyes on my skinny-dipping sessions. A quick swim often helps me relax, so I can sleep when my brain won't shut off. No, I am not ready to tell him any of that.

"Thank you again for joining me. Sorry if I made some of the evening more awkward than necessary. I promise to be better if you would let me give it another try."

I reach up a hand and touch his cheek, and he leans into it. Without thinking, I lift onto my toes to kiss his other cheek. I don't know whether he turns to catch my movement, or it is a matter of fate, but our lips meet. They are closed at first, and the whole experience could just end in an awkward oops, but he opens his lips slightly, and mine follow his lead. Before I can stop myself, my hand leaves his cheek, and my arms go around his neck to pull him down closer. He moans against my mouth, and I completely forget we are virtually strangers standing on my front porch. His arms slide around my back, and the squeaky sound of crushed styrofoam breaks the spell.

I'm not sure who pulls away first, but once again, I wish I was as secure as Shar. My palms itch to touch more than just his handsome face. Other places ache to be touched, and it wouldn't take much coaxing from him for me open the door and invite him upstairs. He is too much of a gentleman, though, and I have already accosted him on my porch. I can't imagine what he is thinking about this half-assed cougar attacking his mouth and then retreating, but when he holds out the bag of food to me, his sheepish grin helps relieve some of the discomfort that is threatening to pool in the pit of my stomach.

"Thank you again for a wonderful time, Asher McNeil. I think I should go on inside now."

An emotion passes across his eyes, but it quickly disappears back to his kind, neutral affect. It might have been disappointment, or maybe that is just me projecting. Either way, I thank him again and take myself inside. As soon as the door closes, the familiar sting hits the backs of my eyes. I can never be the main character. If I hadn't fully accepted it before, I know it now. Maybe he would say no. Maybe he would be disappointed with me. Maybe I'll never know because I just can't take the lead and hold the reins. Shar is half my age, yet she is stronger than I have ever been.

He drives off, and I let the tears fall.

CHAPTER 12
ASHER

The drive home is hazy. I make all the right turns, but I don't remember any of them. All I remember is the way her lips felt on mine. She was liquid heat, and I could've screamed at myself about the stupid food. That was a hell of an interruption. But then she went cold. How does lava freeze mid-stream? What happens in her mind? She left me on the porch again acting like nothing happened when my brain, my hands, my body is still consumed with the touch, taste, and feel of her. If I didn't know any better, I'd think she was young and innocent. Having read a couple chapters in her book, though, I know that she isn't.

I grab the signed novel out of the console and force myself inside the house. I have never been so consumed with a woman I've just met and so confused by her at the same time. Other than after Carolyn's text-message breakup, I've never been uncertain about my feelings for or next steps with a woman. There has to be some way of working through her insecurities, if that's what it is. Maybe she's just really not as into me as she seems. Maybe she's only being nice because I'm the first person who has really talked to her since she arrived. Maybe she'll get out of the house more and decide she no longer wants to be interrupted by the bothersome mailman.

Fuck, she is making me question myself. I'm not going to let any woman have that type of control over my emotions again. I try my best to be a good person, and I genuinely care about other people. Ok, I care about other people except Gabby Brewster. Laughing, I fall onto the sofa and crack open the book in my hand.

I have heard other people, usually girls when I was in college, talk about a book hangover. I don't know if that is what I am feeling, but I know damn well I regret staying up to finish that book last night, or rather, this morning. I couldn't put it down. The characters were so vivid, it was like watching a movie. She is really good at telling a story. She is also very good at describing the intimate moments between her characters. Maybe it is me still reeling from our kiss, but shit, the sex is hot. The main character is assertive and knows what she wants. Though the love interest is no pushover himself, I am drawn to the woman. She wants him, and she shows it unequivocally.

"You're late," Louise yells from behind the delivery bins. I barely stifle a groan.

"Good morning to you too," I say with a yawn.

"Long night with your date?"

"I'm not going to feed the gossip monster, but I'm curious how long it took before you got the call I was out with someone last night."

"I heard she was pretty. A little older but pretty with dark hair."

I groan audibly this time. I should have known. "Let it go,

Louise. I'm not giving you details. I did go out. I enjoyed myself, and then I went home and spent the night reading."

She snorts incredulously, but I'd rather have her not believing what I say than giving any details about Kass to Gabby. Hell, I'm not even going to confirm the identity of my date. The fact Louise is about 20 years older than me and a woman is all that keeps me from flipping her off in response, but my grandmother would jump out of her grave and grab a switch if I did that. It's the only reason I haven't told old Gabby what I think of her, at least not as directly as I'd like to. Instead, I shrug. "Believe what you want." I can feel her eyes rolling at my turned back, but her next question stops me from walking further away.

"What book did you stay up reading, sleepy head?"

Just then, the door chimes with a customer, and I let out a sigh of relief. Only thing is, this customer is more a nightmare than a reprieve. Gabby fucking Brewster. I really am going to have to leave town to get away from her, but I know better than most that leaving town isn't a guarantee.

"Who was reading," she enquires with a syrupy sweetness that turns my stomach.

"Asher said that the reason he was late this morning was because he stayed up all night reading a book." The eye roll is once again evident in her voice, and I feel my hackles rising. I am getting tired of being questioned as if I am a pathological liar.

"You read," Gabby asks, and that is the last straw. I will not let this woman call me dumb on top of everything else.

"Yes, I read. I went to college. I have a degree. Of course, you both know all that and still want to ride my d..." I break off, barely holding myself back from saying something that might come back to haunt me or get me fired. Louise is my supervisor, and she is really laid back, overlooking a lot, like being late on occasion, but our roving manager is not as forgiving. He'd probably get his jollies from firing me. He loves to throw around his authority. Instead of saying anything else, I walk out to my truck. When I come back in, I toss the book on the counter between Gabby and Louise without a word and head back to the small dock to see if there are any deliveries for the day.

They both gasp as I push open the back door, and I pause. Rarely is there anything that catches the two of them off guard. Gabby knows everything, and by default, that means Louise knows it all too. They have grown quiet, and my pulse quickens. Something isn't right.

"Is everything okay," I ask, sticking my head back into the main area through the door?

"Asher." Louise's voice is quiet. Too quiet.

"Where did you get this book?" Gabby's voice screeches through the large space, but her tone is also weird. It isn't quite surprise, but it also isn't incredulity. Is it awe? No, that can't be it. I slowly make my way back toward the counter, my steps tentative, like they could turn around and attack me at any moment.

"Seriously, Asher, this was the book you were reading?" Louise looks flabbergasted when she turns back to face me, the book held almost reverently in her hand.

"Yeah, why? Is it because it's a, what was it called, a romantastic? No, that wasn't it."

"A romantasy," Gabby corrects with an eye roll. For a woman damn near in her 70s, she sure does act like a teenager sometimes.

"Yeah. Why are y'all surprised men might like to read romance, or even romance with their fantasy?"

"That's not it," Louise says. "This book hasn't even been released yet, and here you are with a copy of it. Everyone has been anxiously awaiting its release since the second book in the series came out two years ago. Seriously, Asher, where'd you get this?"

Shit! Why didn't Kass tell me to keep the book hidden?

Why didn't she say it was something everyone would recognize. Then I realize she probably didn't think she would be so well known here in the middle of nowhere. Now what am I going to do.

"You say this is a series?" I pick up the book and flip it over a couple times trying to stall.

Gabby snatches it out of my hands and opens to the first page. "Trials of the Meridien is probably the most waitlisted book at the library. I've had my name down since last year when the publisher announced it would be coming out. And here you are, a clueless man, with a signed copy of the book before publication."

Louise had just taken a sip of her Dr. Pepper and sputters when Gabby mentions the dedication and signature. She quickly grabs the book and opens to the same page it had been on. "I hope you love a good plot twist." Her brows furrow. "What does that mean?" She looks at me expectantly. I can't exactly tell them the truth without giving Kass away as M. Knightsong. From their behavior here, that would likely ruin her solitude up there in her secluded lot. She'd have people camped out on the lawn hounding her for the next book like what happened in that one horror movie about the author who was found by his biggest fan. No, I can't do that to her.

I hate lying, really, I do, but I can see no other way out of this situation. "I was making deliveries one day, and one of our neighbors had a visitor. That visitor happened to be an author, and we got to chatting...as I love to do. I asked her what her books were about, and she told me she writes Romantasy. I asked if she happened to have one of her books I could buy from her and have signed." I try to keep my face neutral. I am, after all, just recounting an experience I had the other day. At least that's what I tell myself to make it through the lies. "This was the only book she had in her car, so she pulled one out and signed it for me before I continued with my deliveries. I finally decided to read it last night."

Gabby scoffs, but Louise eats up my story. I almost feel bad for duping her like that. She's always been direct and honest with me, which is one of the reasons I've kept working with her all these years. "Can I borrow it?" Louise asks with the same level of reverence in her voice she'd had when first holding the book. I'd never imagined a woman in her early 50s would go gaga for a novel. I also never imagined a semi-reclusive gorgeous woman would write romance novels with the steamiest sex scenes.

Before I can let my mind wander in that direction, I feel two sets of eyes boring into me. "I'm sorry." Shit, what do I do?

"Can I read the damn book, Asher?"

"And can I read it after her?"

Fuck, why did Gabby have to be here. I already want to tell Louise no, but I might have considered it less worrisome if she were alone.

Gabby's voice breaks through and tells me I have no choice but to give in. "Why do you seem so reluctant over a book from an author you don't even know. You sure you were telling us the truth?" Her eyebrows nearly reach her widow's peak in question.

"Yeah, sure. Just make sure I get it back. I've never had a signed copy of a book before." I turn away from them and head toward the back again. "I'm going to check for deliveries. Y'all argue over who gets the book first."

CHAPTER 13
KASSANDRA

By the end of the week, Shar was antsy. She hadn't seen the hot surfer who had rocked her world since that night he totally dominated her. Her pussy tightened just thinking about the ways he had taken her and made her want to take him. There's no way it wasn't just as good for him, so why hadn't she seen him? Why hadn't he come back to her room to look for her or even showed up at this end of the beach to surf. It's like he disappeared. She didn't want to think that maybe he had already left town and returned home, if this wasn't his home. She was here for another week for a movie trailer and photo shoot, and she needed to get laid.

Shar scanned the beach, as she had done every day, and her eyes landed on a group of surfers waiting for the perfect wave. Their heads bobbed up and down amidst the undulating waves, and her hopes rose when she noticed a head of wavy blond hair in the group. Was he finally back? Half of the men began paddling toward the shore, moving to stand on their boards, and she pulled her sunglasses back down to cover how intently she was staring in their direction. They looked like their own wave of perfectly formed bodies, and any other day, she'd have been calculating how many of them she could have before the week *was over. Today, however, her eyes locked onto one rider in particular, and the rest of the crowd, on the beach and in the water, melted away.*

His movements were like silk. They were similar to the way he fucked...smooth control. He didn't falter once, not even an ill-timed tremble. He was perfection in the water, and in bed, and she wanted him again. This time, she planned to take control...if she could just get his damn attention.

The men hit the sand and picked up their boards, heading in toward the bar. She pulled her glasses down to make it more obvious she was watching, but he never turned his head. Dammit! What game was he playing? Did he expect her to come to him? That wasn't her style. She turned back toward the waves.

A voice spoke close enough to her ear that she could feel his breath, and her insides turned to mush. "You should learn to go after what you want, Pretty, not just watch it walk by."

"Is that what you do?" She kept herself from looking in his direction, though her entire body was consumed by his nearness.

"Always."

Her spine stiffened at that tiny word. What did that mean if he hadn't sought her out all week. Did that mean he didn't want her? Had he gotten all he wanted? Shit! She knew this was no love match, never intended it to be more than a fun fling, but damn, she didn't expect to be dismissed so quickly. She'd never been dismissed so quickly. She felt, more than heard, him walk away, and she was suddenly cold, though the sun beamed down. Gathering her coverup and beach bag, she headed inside to her room for a hot shower and to find something else to distract her from the thoughts swirling through her mind.

If only I could find something to distract me from my thoughts. I can't help but return to the other night with Asher. So many mixed signals. The fact that he hasn't come around to make any deliveries, though I know I have packages that should have arrived by now, was not helping my mood. Every time I sit down to write, I find myself hoping the doorbell will ring, but it doesn't. I even push back the start time for my writing, hoping he'll interrupt because I miss it, and still, nothing. Now, here I am with my main character steeping in insecurities she's never had before, and I'm frustrated inside.

'You should learn to go after what you want.' The surfer's words play in my mind. I really need to give him a name. If he had a name, I'd be yelling at him to get out of my head right now. I am not going to go into town to search for this man. I'll just wait until he comes back through. And then what, Kass? Are you going to tell him how you've been lusting over him? Are you going to say how you think about him more than you think about your characters? "Stop it," I yell, trying to silence my thoughts. I turn back to my keyboard, ready to pour my emotions onto the page, even if I'm forced to edit them all out later, when the doorbell rings.

A smile explodes across my face, and I nearly float to the entry. I take a moment to wipe my sweaty palms on my lounge pants and get my breath under control before I open the door. As soon as I turn the knob, the door crashes in, and I am crushed in a tight hug from a tiny body.

"Kass!" My sister's enthusiasm overshadows the disappointment that temporarily overtakes my senses. I put my arms around her and squeeze tight, trying to give myself a moment to fix my face before she sees the droop in my smile. I completely forgot she was coming today.

"I'm so glad you made it. Why didn't you call to tell me you were close?"

"I was too excited to get here. Besides, I didn't want you to try and make everything perfect for me. Mom and dad wanted to know how you were really living." I roll my eyes at that. Of course, they do.

"Can I help you bring anything in," I ask, looking out the door to where her car sits in the same spot Asher usually parks his mail truck. Stop thinking about him, Kass. Focus on your sister and her visit now. Get out of your own head. That was so much easier said than done.

Malissa walks toward her car. "I'll grab my bag if you grab the goodies from the front seat." Thoughts of my mom's cookies propel me forward, and I reach into the front passenger side door.

"It's cooler than I thought out here." The words barely leave my mouth when I hear tires on gravel coming up the long driveway.

"Are you expecting someone?" She peeks at me from around the trunk lid.

"No, unless it's the mailman. He's not been up here in a few days, so I might have had some packages come in." I try to keep my voice as neutral as possible while I watch for the familiar truck to appear from between the trees. Still, I feel the jolt of excitement when Asher comes into view.

"Are you going to grab those cookies or not," Malissa's voice breaks my concentration, and I quickly grab up the containers, closing the door to the car. She presses the button on her fob and the doors lock.

"You know you don't have to lock the doors here. There is no one that comes up here."

She jerks her head to the side in the direction of the mail truck and lifts her brow. I shake my head at her and climb the porch steps. I place the containers on the railing that wraps around the porch and wait for Asher to park his truck. He waves, and I can't help but smile. My sister, who has gone inside to drop her bag, returns just as I wave back. She looks back and forth between the two of us, brows furrowed and lips pursed.

"What's going on between you two?"

I scoff. "Nothing. This is a small town, and he delivers all my packages."

"He...brings...you...a...package?" She emphasizes each word, dragging out the last one far longer than necessary.

I glare at her and turn my attention back to the man with his arms full of small boxes and bubble mailers. His eyes catch mine, and his face lights up with that beautiful smile I see in my dreams.

"Good afternoon, Ms. Gingham."

"Nice to see you, Mr. McNeil. Looks like you've gathered quite the collection."

He grins. "Yeah, we had quite an influx of deliveries this week that I haven't been able to make it out here with the small items until today. They piled up a bit, sorry. Where would you like me to put these?"

"Do you mind putting them on the counter?" He doesn't bother to respond, simply crosses the threshold and walks into the sitting area toward the kitchen.

"He knows where to place your mail inside your house?" Malissa asks, barely keeping her voice at a whisper. "What have you not been telling me?"

"Stop it," I whisper-yell back at her, swatting the air.

Asher steps back through the door and pulls up short when he sees Malissa standing next to me. "Oh, I'm sorry. I didn't even see you. Good afternoon." His smile is uncomfortable. Is he embarrassed that he hadn't addressed her on the way in or because we aren't alone?

"Asher McNeill, this is my little sister, Malissa Ross."

"Pleasure to meet you, ma'am." His greeting is so polite that I imagine him tipping his hat had been wearing one.

"The pleasure is all mine," Lissa responds, and I cringe at the slight affectation she uses. Is she flirting or making fun of his accent? Either way, I feel the heat rise up my neck. It isn't jealousy. No, I can't be jealous of Lissa, especially not with a man who isn't mine. Maybe protectiveness. I don't want her hurting his feelings, and sometimes she is unable to read the room.

He turns his attention back to me, and his smile blooms again. "Do you ladies have big plans for the weekend? I'm assuming you didn't just drive out here for dinner," he says, addressing the last part to Malissa.

"No," I begin, thinking to stop him from inviting us out. I want to spend time with him again, but not with my baby sister around.

"My sister isn't much of a planner," Malissa says, and I glare at her again. "If you're from around here, we'd love to hear your suggestions. Is there anything interesting going on in the area this weekend?" I close my eyes and take a couple of deep breaths. That's it. I'm going to have to strangle my own sister.

"Well, there's a great steakhouse if you're looking for dinner. Kass already knows where it is." I see Malissa's brows raise at his use of my nickname. Dammit, why did I tell him to call me that? I'm never going to hear the end of it. "There's also a Dogwood Festival happening over in Youngsville. It's not too far away. So long as you're not allergic, they're beautiful to see in full bloom."

"Oh, both of those sound wonderful! Thank you...Asher, was it?" She is flirting with him.

My back stiffens, and heat creeps up my neck. I'm not sure if I want to throttle Malissa or go cry in my bedroom. Instead, I turn to Asher. "Yes, thank you, Mr. McNeil. I'm sure you have better things to do than play the local welcome center." His smile falls, and I have the urge to reach out and touch his arm, but I hold myself steady.

He recovers quickly, and slaps on a tight smile before responding that he does, indeed, have other deliveries to make before he can head home. He gives a quick 'nice to meet you' to Malissa and a wave to me as he jumps into his truck and takes off down the driveway.

"What in the hell was that, Kassandra?"

"What?"

"It's not like you to dismiss someone so rudely like that. That's my job. What is going on? He was just being nice."

"He is nice," I say quietly, as I grab the cookies on my way in the house.

"No shit, and by the smile that was on his face when he first got here, I'd say he thought you were nice too."

"Stop. You're reading too much into it."

She scoffs and picks up her bag. Looking over her shoulder toward the neatly stacked packages on the counter, she pauses with her foot on the first step heading upstairs. "No mailman carries packages all the way into the house and arranges them neatly for you just because they're nice." With that, she heads upstairs. I think to tell her which room she can stay in, but I figure she'll see the mess in mine and know not to go in that one.

When she is gone, I sit on the recliner and pull my knees to my chest. What the fuck is wrong with me?

CHAPTER 14

KASSANDRA

It is well over an hour before Malissa comes back downstairs. I have long since gotten up from the chair to stretch my legs and find myself in front of my computer screen. I think to pour my frustration into Shar's storyline, much like I had planned to do when Malissa arrived. Instead, I send her to the bar where she meets a young man who has come to the beach with some buddies for the weekend. They are all going to the club down the street from her hotel later, and he invites her to join them.

"What are you working on?" Malissa's voice is soft. I'm not sure if she is trying to gauge my mood or genuinely not wanting to disturb me if I am in the middle of a scene. It sucks that her visit started so tumultuously.

"Working on a scene in this new book I just started a couple of weeks ago."

"Oh yeah, what's it about?"

"It's another one of Shar's adventures."

Malissa walks up and leans back against my desk next to me. "Seriously? That chick hasn't settled down yet?"

I laugh. Shar has always been in control of her feelings and her life. I'm not sure she can picture herself 'settling down' or really settling for anything. She is everything I wish I could be.

"No, she definitely hasn't found the one worth settling for."

"Settling down doesn't mean settling for something less, sis."

Ouch. I am not going to have this conversation. Not today, not after how wrongly this afternoon went.

"Are you hungry?"

"I could eat."

I smile at her. She got that saying from her father. I didn't necessarily like the man when my mom first brought him home to meet me at ten years old. She hadn't necessarily had a great track record with men before that, including my father, so I was skeptical. He has grown on me over the years, and somewhere in my late twenties, I began addressing him as dad rather than Frank. She looks a lot like him, far more than she looks like our mother or me. Mom and I could probably pass for twins most days.

"Okay, let me get dressed, and we'll go get some food somewhere."

"That steakhouse your package deliverer suggested." I stiffen at the reminder of this afternoon. I thought she would let that go after her time upstairs.

"Sure, if that's what you want."

Other than Malissa's explosion of expletives at seeing Brone, our arrival at Country Tavern Steakhouse is uneventful compared to the jealous reception Asher and I encountered. I'm glad. I do not want to have to explain any of that to my sister. In fact, I'd like to forget all of it, but I can't. Instead, I focus my attention on the menu. There is no way we are ordering as much food tonight as Asher had ordered the last time. No doubt, there were still leftovers in my fridge. That thought immediately brought to mind our kiss and how awkwardly it ended because of those containers...because of me.

"Are you okay?" Malissa's worried look brings me out of the emotional hole I am digging. There is no need to be so emotional, not for someone I have just met. It's silly.

"Yeah. I just thought of something in my book that wasn't working."

She looks skeptical. Thankfully, the server arrives in time to save me from whatever thoughts are percolating in Malissa's mind. We go ahead and place our orders. Mine includes a glass of wine, and she goes for a local IPA. I didn't even know the town had a local brewery. Before the server leaves, we order our food, agree to share a small sampler platter and an appetizer. I, of course, make sure the meat sampler includes a small ribeye. My mouth salivates thinking about it. Then I think about Asher's response to my enjoying the steak here last time, and my lips curl into a smile.

"What is going on with you?" Though her tone isn't quite accusatory, I feel the accusation, and heat creeps up my neck to my ears. Thankfully, I have worn my hair down tonight. I'm not about to tell my baby sister that I am thinking of how much Asher enjoys my food orgasm faces. I'd never hear the end of that.

"Nothing. You know my brain is never quiet."

"Yeah, no shit, but you usually hide it a little better in public. You're always so cautious. Tonight, you look like your emotions are on a light switch, and someone keeps flipping it."

"No happy medium on the dimmer switch, huh?"

"Nope. Ecstasy and despair all the way. Are you writing a book in your head or is it something else?'

"I'm fine, Lissa. Seriously."

"You've lived here for a year, and the only person who comes to see you is the mailman." Her eyebrows nearly touch her hairline by the end of that statement, and I am torn between crying at the truth of it and laughing at her expression. I opt for laughing.

"Ouch..."

"Kassandra, right?" An older voice comes up behind me, saving me from having to continue my response to Malissa's astute observation.

"Jerry. So good to see you again."

"Asher didn't come with you this time?" I take a quick sip of my water, trying to staunch the blush quickly filling my cheeks. I catch Malissa's smirk, and nearly throw my napkin at her.

"No, sir. This is my sister Malissa. She came to visit me for the weekend, and I knew she would love the food here."

"I'm so glad to hear that. Hold on a sec." He looks over his shoulder and calls out. "Jeanie."

"Is she feeling better now?" I turn in my seat to see a middle-aged white woman with curly, flame-red hair who looks closer to my age of 45 than Jerry's making her way to our table with a huge smile on her face.

"Yeah. Even if she wasn't, I can't keep her out of this place for long," he says, eyes lighting up more the closer she gets. The woman slips her arm around his waist as she smiles down at us. "Ladies, this is my Jeanie. She's the reason this place even exists. Jeanie, this is Asher's friend Kassandra I told you about the other day. She's new around here, and this," he says, gesturing toward Malissa, "is her sister who is visiting for the weekend."

"It's so nice to have you ladies here. Please make sure you try a piece of our pies on me." Jerry looks at me with a wink, and I cover my mouth to hide the giggle that bubbles up.

"Thank you so much, Jeanie," I say in a halted response as I get myself together. "That's very nice of you. What we'd love is to hear the story of how you all started this place. Asher told me there's a fun history of this building and Brone."

"Oh my, yes." She looks up at Jerry with such warmth, I am doubly sure I want to include this place and these two people in my next book. They lock fingers for a moment, and then she turns back to us. "Do you mind if we sit?"

"Not at all," Malissa says, jumping out of her seat to come sit next to me before I can respond. I can't help but smile at her enthusiasm.

"We're not as young as we once were, or at least not as young as we were when we fell in love with this place." Jerry's voice takes on a storytelling resonance that draws me in. Our food comes, and we hardly touch it while this beautiful couple tells us their love story, what brought them to the middle of nowhere, and how they came to own the building and Brone as a packaged deal.

"I never thought to find love in my early forties, don't let the hair color fool you, and then fall in love with the countryside," Jeanie adds in conclusion to their story. "We were city folk. Then we took that drive, and saw this barn..."

"And that's what it was at the time, nothing more than a barn," Jerry pipes in.

"We had talked about starting a business together and taking a chance on us. This place was the perfect location for a restaurant being right off the interstate."

"All it took was her beautiful eyes and a sweet kiss for me to make an offer to the owners who still own all the land down the hill and across the valley. They couldn't believe we wanted this land and barn they'd left in disuse. I told them we'd take it 'as is,' and within the week, we owned the land with this building and everything inside."

"What the previous owners didn't know was that one of their bulls had made its way out here and was living its best life in the barn. We walked in, and there he was munching hay that had been here for who knows how long, at least a few years." Her laughter rings through the restaurant. "Jerry, I think we've stayed here too long. Our friends' food is probably cold already."

"No, no, this has been great," I say, and I mean it. "Your story is so sweet, and I love how you just happened to find Brone and made him the mascot of your restaurant."

"Oh yeah, people come from all over the state to take their picture with him. Jerry asks that they send us a copy of their photos, so we can hang them here in the restaurant. I'm sure you saw them in the foyer."

"No, I missed that," Malissa exclaims, jumping out of her seat and walking back toward the entrance. The three of us laugh, and I thank them again for sharing their time and story with us.

They rise from the table, grabbing our server's attention. "Be sure our friends here each get a free piece of pie." The server nods with a smile, and everyone goes on about their business. I take another bite of my cooled steak and enjoy its juicy savoriness, then nearly choke when I hear Malissa's voice followed by Asher's. My body warms at its timbre. Why do I recognize his voice from across a busy room, and why in the hell does my body respond to it?

CHAPTER 15
ASHER

For years, I've said I would not let another woman fuck with my emotions again, but damn if my emotions don't feel fucked with. We're not a couple. We're nothing but a couple of strangers who, I think, happen to be attracted to one another. Maybe our kiss was a fluke, or maybe it might have sparked something more, but the way she acted this afternoon, I just don't know.

I wish I would have brought my own truck out for deliveries today. I have no desire to go back into town, and even less desire to deal with Louise and Gabby. Louise isn't so bad. She'll be about ready to lock up, but if Gabby is still there, we'll never get out of the building.

Thankfully, the lobby lights are off when I arrive, so I pull into the parking lot and let myself in the back door. "Louise?" I hear her muffled response from the other room, closest to the front counter and make my way out of the delivery area. "Hey, need any help closing up?"

"Yeah, we had a huge rush at the end of the day."

"Really?" Though it's not unheard of for people to stop by the post office on their way home from work, we almost never have what I would call a rush. This town is too small for that. When I come around the back wall, though, I find Louise digging through the large cart, pulling out all the mail we received today. "All of this right before closing?" My tone must have been more skeptical than I meant to sound because she looks up at me sharply. Then I see a glint in her eye.

"I may have lost track of time trying to finish that book and didn't get the mail separated earlier." She shrugs sheepishly.

"You mean, you spent the whole day reading and just dropping whatever came in here in this bin and forgot about it." I can't help but laugh. "The book was that good, huh? I'm surprised Gabby isn't still here talking your ear off."

"That's why I rushed to finish it. She wouldn't leave me alone. As soon as I turned the last page, she snatched it out of my hand and ran off. I'll be surprised as hell if she doesn't return it to you in the morning."

Together, we pull the last of the mail out of the bin and sort it, so it will be ready to go out on the first trucks to arrive in the morning. I admit that the busyness is good for me. It helps clear my head much more than going home and wallowing in self-doubt would have. I am not going to do that, not again.

"So, you asked me about how good the book was. How about we head down to the steakhouse for some beers and talk about it? I'm curious about your thoughts since you've never read anything of hers before."

Louise's offer takes me by surprise. Though we have worked together for a few years now, we don't really hang out outside of the office. She usually goes straight home to do whatever she does at home, and I go my separate way. Occasionally, we both head to the bar down the street here for a beer after a particularly trying day, usually one when the boss comes to town, but that's it.

"Sure. I have no other plans, and I'm hungry anyway."

I forget it's Friday night, so when we arrive at the steakhouse, the place is hopping with a line out the door. A bunch of families with smaller children are hanging around Brone's pen watching him eat while they wait for their tables. I see Jeanie outside talking to the hostess.

"Hey, Jeanie, feeling better?"

"Asher," she says, greeting me with a hug. "Much better! I told Jerry it was just a bug, but he was clucking around me like a mother hen." For self-proclaimed city slickers, they both have picked up so many of our euphemisms that constantly have me laughing.

"It's great to see this place so busy on a Friday night. Louise and I were hoping to find a couple seats at the bar."

"Yes, business is good." Her smile spreads. "Go on in, and check for yourselves. Good to see you, Louise." She holds the door open for us, allowing us to bypass the line of waiting customers.

I love Jeanie and Jerry as if they were my own grandparents. Unlike the rest of the townsfolk who blamed me for the breakup with Carolyn and her subsequent poor choices, they never did. When my father, and then my grandmother passed, they checked in on my mom while I was away at college. After I came home and took over as mom's full-time caregiver, they watched out for me too. My first job after I came home had been in this very restaurant. They would let me work a few short shifts, and Jeanie would go sit with mom. I can never fully repay their kindness, so I do my part to direct all visitors and newcomers out here. The food and service will always be enough to keep them coming back.

"Look at that," Louise exclaims. "Two spots waiting for us."

She takes the spot at the end of the bar and immediately orders a Cadre, leaving me to squeeze my big self in between her and someone else. I haven't had one of those beers since I was a teen when we would all get an older friend to go buy us the cheapest thing available and have a bonfire in the woods. Just thinking about that time made me send up a quick prayer of thanks that we all survived those days. I order a local IPA and some smoked jalapeño sausage.

Louise turns in her seat, knees against my thighs. "So, what did you think of the book? Wasn't it great?" I have never seen her so animated. At work, she's like a robot going through the motions. This is a different side of her, like she's lost a decade just by dropping the stuffy exterior. I laugh.

"Do you want my opinion, or do you just want me to agree with you?" I absolutely did like it, particularly because I spent the whole night picturing the author as the main character and me as the love interest. That sounds so ridiculous just thinking it, but it's true. Louise slaps my shoulder, jolting me back into the moment.

"Your opinion, Asher."

"I enjoyed it. It's not the first romance novel I've read, Louise. Remember that I came back home to a house of women. There were plenty of old timey romance novels with the long-haired muscle men on the covers hidden around the place." Her eyes go wide. "What? You thought my grandmother a prude?"

"Um, I, um, I didn't think of her much at all, except in the most respectful way. She was a pillar of the community."

"Yes, that she was. And she also had a bag full of those books hidden under the nightstand by her bed." I laugh as her mouth opens and closes like a fish. If only she knew how confused I had been when I found them cleaning out the house over the years. I bet she'd be less surprised to know I found a trunk full of Hustlers in the barn. Whether they were my grandfather's or my father's, I don't know.

Considering neither couple had more than one child, it seems like they spent more time reading, or in the case of the men, looking at pictures, than they spent doing the things they read about.

"Asher?"

An unfamiliar voice sounds behind us, and I have to wait for Louise to turn, so that I can pry myself out of the tight barstool. My jaw drops at the sight of Kassandra's sister. Though I hadn't spent much time with her, or even looked at her fully, I'd have recognized her. They favor. The same almond-shaped eyes, and thick, wavy hair, though Kassandra's is a richer dark brown.

"It's Malissa, Kassandra's sister."

"Yes, I remember you. I was just surprised to see you here."

"Yeah, this was such a great recommendation."

She must have noticed Louise staring at her with curiosity because she finishes with an apology for interrupting us. Louise scoffs, and I shake my head. This is going to be a fiasco.

"We're just unwinding after work. Nothing really to interrupt." Louise is cordial enough, but her eyes bore into me with the question I do not want to answer—Who is Kassandra?

I look out beyond where Malissa stands, and I find her immediately. She is in one of the large tables by the window. They must have gotten here early before the crowd to get such prime real estate, unlike us, ok me, scrunched up here like a sardine. She is looking this way, though I'm not sure whether it is to find her sister or something else, so I wave just in case. I know better with Louise sitting next to me, but I can't pretend like I don't see her. When she waves back shyly, I feel Louise puff up, and I know this will not remain a quiet night.

"Why don't you two join us? We have plenty of room." Malissa is obviously the more outgoing of the sisters because Kass looks like she wants to crawl under the table as soon as we stand and begin walking that way.

"Kass, look who I found up there at the bar. The friendly, neighborhood mailman."

"Good evening, Asher." Her tone is formal and distant. I hate it, but I can see her eyes taking in Louise, and I understand.

"This is my coworker…"

"Supervisor."

"Supervisor," I say with a roll of my eyes that has Malissa laughing aloud, "Louise." Though the corners of her mouth tick up a bit, Kass maintains her serious demeanor. "Louise, this is Kassandra Gingham."

"From the big house down on Hampshed," she says excitedly and slides into a seat like a child waiting for story time. I mouth an apology, but Kass just turns a resigned look toward Louise.

"Have you all ordered your food already?" She asks, and I realize I forgot all about my meal.

"I'll be right back. Let me go tell the bartender where we ran off to."

I take note of what the sisters are drinking, and I order each of us another round while I'm up there. It's the least I can do to compensate for the mess this night has just become. When I get back to the table with our drinks, I find Louise and Malissa in animated conversation about books of all things. Kassandra is pretending to sip her wine, which is pretty much gone. I trade glasses with her, and the smile she gives me warms my insides.

"Looks like they've become fast friends," I say, unable to think of anything else to say.

"Yeah, bonding over books will do that."

"I need some fresh air. Would you like to join me while I wait for my food? That is if you were finished eating."

"Yes, please." Her response is quiet enough for me to hear, and I hold out my hand. Neither of the other two women seem to notice, so we sneak out the side door without a backward glance.

"Hey," I start, wanting to warn her about Louise and her yet unreleased book, but she doesn't give me a chance.

"I'm sorry about this afternoon. I was extremely rude, and I feel terrible about it." I freeze. I need to catch my breath from the wave of heat that rushes over me. She is apologizing. I've honestly never had a woman apologize for her behavior before. I take her hands, making sure we are out of direct eye shot from the table.

"You don't need to apologize. Your sister was there to visit, and I was interrupting."

"No, you were just being your wonderfully nice self. I don't know what came over me, but I…"

I kiss her. I hadn't intended to kiss her. I definitely didn't invite her outside to kiss her, but the look of contrition on her face coupled with her apology is more than I can stand. It only lasts a second before I come back to my senses and pull away fully expecting her stinging slap to follow. Instead, she puts her arms around my neck and pulls my mouth back to hers. What starts as an uncertain meeting of lips fans into a frenzy. My hands are in her hair, her tongue is in my mouth, and when she pulls my lip between her teeth, I growl.

"If you keep that up, the live band won't be the only show these people will get tonight."

She seems to sober at my statement, but she doesn't pull away. A cheer rises inside me, and I smile widely. She must feel the change because she lifts her lips from mine and looks up at me. A smile plays on the sides of her mouth too, and then we both bust out laughing, untangling our fingers from hair and arms from around each other.

"No styrofoam this time," I say, planting a chaste kiss at the corner of her upturned mouth. She giggles. Then she pulls my ear down to her mouth, and the heat of her breath has me needing to readjust my pants again.

"The next time you growl at me, make sure we're not in public." And with that, she turns to walk back toward the door. I grab her hand, trying to get control of my cock that has just drained all the blood from my brain.

"Wait. Wait. I asked you out here for a reason." Her look of confusion nearly has me laughing again. "No, what just happened was an unexpected bonus."

"Oh."

I cup her cheek, turning her face back up to mine. "Trust me that I wanted to kiss you. I've been wanting to kiss you. But I brought you out here to warn you that…"

Malissa came crashing out the door, and rushed right at me, her finger pointing at my chest. "You gave her unreleased book away for others to read." It isn't a question. "Are you dumb?"

"Lissa, what are you doing?"

"Louise just asked me if I had read anything by M. Knightsong. Then she said she managed to get her hands on Trials of the Meridien. Since I know the only person with a direct line to the author was this big lug, I put two and two together."

If I hadn't already released Kassandra's arm at Malissa's initial accusation, the look of confusion and disappointment on Kass' face would have knocked me away. "That's what I was trying to tell you." I put my hands up. "I didn't know…I mean…I knew the book was unreleased, but I didn't really know what that meant. I knew you got the box, and when you signed it to me, I didn't know." Her eyes soften slightly, but Malissa's do not. I choose to ignore Malissa. "I made the mistake of telling Louise and Gabby that I had stayed up all night reading, and they asked me what book. I brought it in the post office, and they both went crazy, asking where I'd gotten it, and how I'd gotten it signed. I didn't want to give you away, so I told them it was some random person I met making deliveries. At that point, I had to let them borrow it. I'm sorry."

"You didn't want to give her away, but you give her work away...free...to be shared around town?"

"That's enough, Lissa. Go back inside. Tell her we're on our way back in." Malissa huffs in a way only younger siblings can do, but then she turns and walks back inside, a false smile plastered on her face. "My sister is very protective of me. There have been incidents. They were early in my career, but they were scary. Anyway, I understand why you did what you did. Hopefully, it goes no further than the two of them reading it and giving it back to you."

This time, when she walks away, I let her go. I take a few deep breaths before I follow her back into the restaurant. By then, they are putting on their jackets and saying their farewells. I sigh and wave goodbye at their backs before I sit down to the food I no longer want.

CHAPTER 16

KASSANDRA

The shower did nothing to improve Shar's mood. The silkiness of the suds running over her breasts and down between her thighs had her hornier and more frustrated than she was when he left her sitting on the beach. Fuck him! There were plenty of other men around to take care of her needs.

Hair pulled back into a chic bun, she looked at herself in the mirror and dropped her towel to the floor. She pulled on one of her slinkiest cocktail dresses, letting the fabric slide over her skin like liquid silver, the chain-like straps clinking against her earrings as they fell into place. The cool color was a striking contrast against her tanned skin, and it fell just low enough to cover her thong. She finished the look off with black stilettos and a black clutch. She was not ending the night alone.

Her first stop was the bar by the lobby. Time to pre-game with a couple of tequila shots before heading to the clubs down the strip. It barely took fifteen minutes before men began approaching, asking her name, and offering to buy her a drink. Most of them were much older, even older than the surfer who would not get out of her head, so she smiled and then ignored them. She was looking for different energy tonight.

"Where's the party?" A melodious voice came from her left.

Though she was getting ready to leave, she gave him a once over and decided that he might be worth delaying her departure for a few minutes. She licked her lips and took the final sip of her drink. "I heard there's a couple of fun spots down the strip. I thought I'd hit them up and see what's happening."

His dark eyes took her in slowly from head to toe before he invited her to join him and his friends as they bar hop the strip. Apparently, it was a wedding weekend, and he was the only one there without a significant other. Or at least that was his story. She didn't believe him for a heartbeat, and for all she knew, he was the groom-to-be, but she also didn't care. He looked safe and like he'd be fun for the night. That was all she wanted.

Though she had planned to grab a for-hire ride to the furthest spot on the strip and work her way back toward her hotel, the group had decided to go the other direction. It was inconvenient, but she wasn't bothered. So long as she didn't end the night alone, a longer ride there or back would not matter. His group consisted of three other couples who all looked like they were barely out of college. She didn't bother learning anyone's name because she had no intentions of seeing any of them again after tonight.

"So do you live here?" one of the guys asked, his date clinging to his arm like she was either too drunk to stand already or she was afraid he would disappear should she let him go.

"No, I'm just here for the week." She wasn't going to tell them that she was here for work because then they would want more details. They always wanted more details. The only person who hadn't wanted more details left her sitting alone and frustrated on a lounge chair this afternoon. She shook her head to clear those thoughts, grabbed her drink from the bar, a Long Island this time, and made her way to the dance floor. She was going to get that man out of her head.

"Do you mind if I join you?" her dark-eyed date asked, grabbing her around the waist. She put her arms around his neck, making sure not to spill any of her drink on his shirt. He

pulled her tight against his torso, and as they moved to the music, she felt the stirrings of his arousal. It wasn't going to be a life-changing night, but it'd do.

By the time they got to the second bar, most of the girls in their group, were pissy drunk, each taking on a different persona. There was the complainer who just wanted to go back to the hotel, a crier, and the horny bitch whose date spent most of the night trying to keep her hands out of his pants. He should've just taken her in the bathroom and gotten it out of her system. Shar couldn't help but think that they'd all have been much happier.

At the last bar, Shar and her date were the only ones left, and he kept throwing hints that they head to his hotel room. The longer they had spent together with his friends, and the more he drank, the less interested she was in spending the night with him. When he went to the bathroom for the fourth time, she considered hailing a for-hire, but she felt guilty since he was still out alone because of her. So, she turned to the bar, and ordered herself a soda. One of them needed to drink less.

"What are you doing at this end of the strip, pretty?"

Her breath caught, as that silky smooth voice washed over her. She tried to ignore him, but his hand was on her bare hip, her dress having crept up as she sat on the barstool. She felt the roughness of his hands kneading the flesh of her upper thigh, and her panties were instantly drenched. My god, he had some kind of spell over her body. The bartender set her drink down and looked between the two of them. His knitted brows drawing her out of the trance this man's hands were weaving around her.

She turned to face him. "I'm here with my date."

He smirked. "Oh really, and where is this date of yours?"

"In the restroom, if you must know. We were getting ready to head back to the hotel."

A darkness crept across his face before he blinked it away and laughed, looking at the new drink she had just ordered. Still, he nodded in acquiescence and walked away, blending into the crowd around the dance floor. Goosebumps formed on her bare arms and legs, as if he had taken all of her heat with him, like maybe he was heat itself.

"Sorry, I took so long," her nearly forgotten date said, leaning on the bar beside her. His words were slurring, and his lean was probably more from necessity than charm. She had started the night sure she would end it getting all her needs met, but she had no desire to take advantage of a drunk kid who suddenly made her feel old at the ripe age of twenty-three.

"Thank you for a very nice time. It was great to meet you and your friends, but I think it's time I get some sleep."

"What do you mean? The night is young, and so are we." He grabbed her arm and spun the stool around, so she was facing him. He placed his knee between her thighs before she realized what was happening. His face was inches away from hers, and his hand was running up her thigh.

"What are you doing?" She tried to push his hand away and turn herself, so she was at least facing the bar directly, but he held her in place, his knee brushing her panties.

"Look at you, wet for me already." His hand squeezed her thigh until she squealed, and he laughed. "I bet you like it rough, don't you." She was shaking her head. This cannot be happening in a busy bar, at the bar, with all these people around.

"Let me go." She said it as directly as she could while trying not to draw too much attention, but he closed the distance, trying to kiss her. She turned her head just in time, so his tongue grazed her chin instead, and she recoiled. His breath was putrid, as if he had just vomited in the bathroom. She put her hands up to push him away, but he was stronger than her, even in his drunken state, and he pushed her back into the seat, her arm bumping the guy on the stool next to her. Why hadn't they left when his friends had. Why hadn't she left when he was in the bathroom.

Finally, the person sitting next to her turned around and shouted, "What the hell, dude?"

He looked up at him with a sneer. "Mind your bus..." His

sneer turned to a whimper, as a hand came from behind Shar and clamped onto his wrist, bending his hand back.

"I suggest you remove your other hand from her before I remove it completely." There was venom in the tone, but she'd have recognized that voice anywhere.

The guy slowly lifted his right hand from her thigh. "Get off of me," Shar yelled, trying to push his knee from between her legs. She didn't have to push hard because her surfer turned her stool slightly and dragged the guy away from her and onto the floor. He was crying at this point from the pressure of his wrist still being twisted in an awkward position.

"Please. Please. I'm sorry. I didn't mean anything by it. I thought she was into it."

"When a woman tells you to let her go, turns away from you, pushes you away, you listen, you little prick." He dragged the kid outside and put him in a taxi. She was glad she could see them through the window because she was afraid he was going to do much worse. She watched for the surfer to come back into the bar while a group of women gathered around asking if she was okay. She was not okay.

"Are you ready to leave now, pretty?" His voice was little more than a whisper in her ear. She nodded silently and grabbed her bag from the bar. She put her arms around his waist and let him lead her outside.

"It's Shar," she said quietly. When he didn't respond, she repeated, "My name is Shar, not pretty."

He led her to a black sports car that was parked outside the bar. His finger under her chin, he lifted her face to look at him. "I call you pretty because you are, and I like the way you respond when I say it. Now you're shaking, so let's get you warmed up." He opened the car door and let her in before he climbed in behind the wheel on the other side.

I don't know how long I sit staring at my screen before Malissa comes down the stairs asking about coffee. She knows I hate coffee, but she has to ask anyway. It's a thing between us.

"Are you okay, sis?"

I sniff, trying to control the shiver that has taken over my body. "Yeah. I just wrote a tough scene where Shar was almost assaulted." The last word comes out with a sob.

"Hey," Malissa says, rubbing my shoulders. "She will be fine. You are safe. There is no one here but us."

"The guy swore she wanted it because she hung out with him and had a few drinks. It all happened so fast." Tears stream down my face. "He said I wanted it because I wrote smut. Since I write about it, I must want to do it." I turn and bury my face in my sister's midsection, my arms around her waist as unwanted memories flood through my mind.

"Kass, you're safe. Shar is safe. You are home. You would not leave her in that position. You are fine. Everything is fine."

We stay like that for what seems like hours before my tears stop, and I begin to feel like myself again. Malissa steps out of my arms to give me space, like she's done so many times over the years, but she runs her fingers through my hair, maintaining contact. Instinctively, she knows what to do to help me relax and come back to the present.

I've never written a scene where Shar is potentially in danger. She knows how to take care of herself, knows the safe places to go, and is very selective with the men she spends time with. I don't know what triggered this momentary lapse for her, and me, but I need it to be a one and done situation. I need her to remain strong and undamaged. I need her to be everything I'm not.

"I think I'm good now, Lissa." I walk to the kitchen and

pull out the secret stash of coffee pods I had ordered when she said she was coming to visit. I still hate coffee, but she has earned a cup. Grabbing my phone to look at the time while the coffee runs through the machine, I notice a missed message from Asher. I look up at Malissa who is busily scrolling through her own phone, and quickly open the message.

> Asher: Hey, I realized I never told you that I really enjoyed the book.

> Asher: The story was great and held my interest all the way through. I did say I stayed up all night reading it, and that was the truth.

> Asher: Before I start rambling and gushing about how much I enjoyed some of the scenes, I'll end this message here.

> Asher: Just wanted to say thank you for the book and that I did really like it.

"What are you smiling at?"

I jump, nearly dropping my phone into the sink. Lissa's eyebrow greets her hairline at my clumsy fumbling. I feel heat entering my cheeks and laugh, trying to cover up the flush, but she is having none of it.

"I'm guessing it's a text message from a certain ginger in uniform."

"Today is Saturday. I doubt he's in uniform."

"Gotcha!"

Dammit, I walked right into that one. "He sent a text to tell me that he liked the book. Of all the things we talked about..." I have to clear my throat to get past the word talked. "He hadn't told me what he thought of the book." Instead, I think to myself, his lips told me what he thought of me. Again, the familiar warmth washes over me, but this time it travels down to my stomach. I quickly put my phone down on the counter and change the subject. "So, what do you want to do today?"

She smiles knowingly. No one can read me as well as Lissa, and it has never been as annoying as it is now. Even when we were kids, well, when she was a kid, she somehow knew when I had done something that wasn't allowed, I didn't mind because she never told on me. Her outburst of protectiveness from last night, though, made me wonder how she would react if she really knew what I thought and felt about Asher.

"Let's go to that festival your big mouth mailman told us about. It sounded fun."

"Who are you, and what have you done with my sister?"

"What do you mean?" My lips purse, and my eyebrows speak for me at the inconsistency between her bouncy question and the sly grin on her face. She is up to something.

"You know damn well that fairs and festivals that likely have lots of children around have never been your thing."

"True, but this is different." I walk around the counter toward her and cross my arms. "No, it is. I've never been out here. So, I get to see new things on the drive, and I, realistically, never have to see these people again." The little flick of her wrist, as she adds flourish to her final point has me rolling my eyes, but I let it go. I am not going to get a different answer from her, at least not today.

"Fine. Let me take a shower and get ready."

CHAPTER 17
ASHER

I don't sleep well. My mind keeps replaying the events from last night. So much happened, and yet, nothing has changed. I am still as confused by Kass as I have been for the past week. I can't say what compelled me to finally knock on her door to check on her after having delivered out there for months. I mean, the packages always disappeared, so it should have been obvious that someone lived in the house. I guess curiosity finally got the best of me.

Then I saw her disoriented from the interruption, with her silky nightgown and robe, and my mouth went dry. She was stunning. I'd have come back a hundred times just to look into her hazel eyes or catch a glimpse of those gloriously thick thighs. I was surprised at how cordial she was when I interrupted her again the next day. I figured she'd tell me to go to hell, but she didn't. She seemed just as interested, but then things went awkward.

She turned cold and ran away into the house like a scared rabbit. If I was more of a hunter, I might have followed her, but I don't generally chase after women who don't want to be caught. Yet, something keeps taking me back to her door, and every day, she lets me get a little closer before she pulls away.

It's the most deliciously frustrating feeling, this cat and mouse game we seem to be playing.

So, when she kissed me last night, I saw stars, literal stars. Her mouth was so warm and inviting. And then she leaned into me, curving that lush body along mine, and I wanted to devour her. I spend all night still imagining what it would be like to touch her, taste her. The grandfather clock chimes 6am at the same time my cock twitches for the umpteenth time. Shit, I need to get up and take a shower. I reach for the phone and text Louise.

> I'm already up and getting ready. I'll take the early shift this morning.

> Louise: On a Saturday? Be my guest. See you at 10.

I chuckle to myself at her surprise. Saturdays are usually my days for sleeping in, even more than Sundays. Something about not having to work at all has me awake and excited for the day. I wonder whether Kass and her sister have anything exciting planned for their day as I step into the old clawfoot tub and turn on the shower. Big men should never have to step into small tubs with shower heads that barely reach their chin, I think to myself as the water begins to warm the air around me. Surely, at least one of the bathrooms in that big house Kass has all to herself has a decent shower.

My cock responds with another hardening twitch at the idea of being in the shower with Kass. The image of her hardening nipples when I growl at her pushes me to take my cock in hand. Stroking it from base to hilt, I remember the feel of her lips on mine, and the way that she pulled my face down to hers with her hands around my neck. When she bites my lip in the memory, I am lost, my hand working short strokes, building until I hear myself moan. *The next time you growl at me, make sure we're not in public.* Those words running through my brain push me over the edge, and I nearly collapse onto the rim of the tub with the force of my release. Shit, I have it bad for that woman.

I never work Saturday mornings, so I never realized how damn slow things are during the early hours. By the time I usually come in, there is a steady stream of people dropping off mail, or at least coming in to check their PO Boxes, something to break up the time and make it seem to go faster. Whenever Louise comes in, I'll tell her that she never has to worry about me taking the early shift again. I'll gladly close things out.

During one particularly slow spell, I remember that I never told Kass my opinion of the book she gave me. I look through my text threads until I find the unnamed one and open it. The selfie we took at the steakhouse spreads warmth through my chest. If anyone were to walk through the door at that moment, they'd swear I'm losing my mind because of the huge smile on my face. I send a quick text telling her that I really liked it. I don't want to go into too much detail on what I liked about it, or the images her words created in my mind, but I want her to know I enjoyed it. She doesn't respond right away, so I think maybe she is still asleep, although she always claims early morning is her favorite writing time.

Twenty minutes later, just as Louise walks in the door, my phone chimes.

> Kassandra: Hey, we're thinking of going to that dogwood festival you told us about. Would you like to go?

My heart skips a beat, and my face must show my

excitement because Louise asks if I'm alright. I'm better than alright.

"Yeah, I'm good. Now that you're here, I'm going to put together the deliveries, and if there are enough, I'll go ahead and take them, so they're not sitting here the whole weekend. We've been slow anyway."

She shrugs. "Saturday mornings are always slow. That's why I like being here. I can read, or just sip my coffee in peace and quiet. Gabby isn't even out and about that early."

I laugh. I still don't understand the friendship between these two women, and I probably never will, but I'm not going to worry about that. There are more important things to think about, like how I can change my clothes and get to Kass' house preferably before they leave for the festival. I walk to the back and quickly send a response.

> Hey, yeah, I'd love to go. I'm at work right now, but I could pick y'all up at 12:30.

> Kassandra: Why don't you just meet us there? What time do you think you'd make it? Give me a place to be for you to find us.

> Oh ok. How about at the Merry Go Round at 1?

> Kassandra: Sounds great. We'll see you then.

I have never been so glad to hear customers come through the door as I am right then. I don't need Louise watching me walk on cloud nine. I am not good at lying, and now that she's met Kass and her sister, she's more than likely to figure out why I have a huge smile on my face and am dancing around between the bins. As I put together the deliveries, I know the next two hours are going to fly by.

CHAPTER 18

KASSANDRA

If I thought my house was in the middle of nowhere, it is nothing compared to the small villages and sparse homesteads we pass on our way to Youngsville. I am beginning to think we will find this festival in the middle of a field rather than a town.

"I don't think I ever realized the true meaning of rural before this trip, sis."

Rather than a laugh, a tiny puff of air comes out of my nose in response to her statement. We've always had such similar thought patterns.

"Seriously, this place makes your street look like the suburbs."

This time I do laugh, and I watch the corner of her mouth tick up in a smile. My shoulders relax, and the tension from this morning's writing session completely melts away. Malissa has always been able to bring me back to baseline when my emotions have gotten out of hand. I won't tell her, but I've needed this distraction. I've needed some sister time.

"Hey," she said, turning her whole body toward me. I stiffen slightly knowing that she is going to ask something I don't want to answer. That's always how she starts deep conversations. When I don't say anything, she barrels on.

"Are you going to make it home for mom and dad's anniversary? You know they miss you and would really like you to be there. It's going to be a whole thing, and I don't want to have to go through it all alone. Please."

Even if I want to interject, she doesn't come up for air until she gets it all out.

"Are you finished?"

"Please Kassie." She has been the only one to ever call me Kassie, and now she only uses it when she really wants something.

"I can't answer that any other way than to say I will try." She pushes out her bottom lip and turns back to face the window. "Lissa, don't act like that. Let's just enjoy the day. Then, before you leave, you give me all the information, and I will do my best. Can that be enough?"

"Fine, but I really hope that by your best, you find a way to make it." We fall into another uncomfortable silence for the remainder of the trip. I spend most of it biting the skin inside my lip. Thankfully, we crest a hill overlooking a rather large town before my lip starts bleeding.

"Look, Lissa, civilization." She is already taking in the view, but I needed to break the silence. I want her smiling again. Hell, I want to smile again.

"Ooh, I see a ferris wheel." Finally, her excitement overtakes the melancholy, and she nearly bounces in her seat. Even at almost 30 years old, she is still child-like sometimes.

"I am not riding the ferris wheel."

"Oh c'mon, Kass. It's safe, and you can obviously see the entire town from up there." She spreads her hands wide in exaggeration. When I look in her direction, she is holding her breath, trying to hold back the mirth for so long that her face has turned red. Not for the first time today, my eyes roll at her.

I pull into the first empty parking space I find, which is

still a couple blocks from the amusement rides we saw. There are dogwood trees along both sides of the entire Main Street, and they are all in full bloom. The view is spectacular, almost like a row of parade floats down the street.

"No wonder they have a dogwood festival here each year," I say, gesturing toward the rows of trees. Lissa nods her head in solemn agreement. After taking a few minutes to admire the blooms, we walk in the direction of the cacophony of music, voices, and games that can only mean the fair is in town.

"Omigosh, I'm so hungry!" Lissa's eyes light up the closer we get.

I roll mine. "We just ate lunch before we left."

"Yeah, but funnel cake!" We both laugh and walk faster.

⁂

I look at Lissa from the corner of my eye. Something is going on with her. This is the fourth time we have circled around the center of the festival to the merry-go-round, and she keeps looking at her watch. We skip by so many vendors, and I have yet to find a restroom after our huge drinks and sugar binge.

"What's going on? What's your obsession with this part of the festival?"

"What? Oh. Nothing. I just want to ride this thing, but the line is always so long."

She says the words with the proper enthusiasm, but she doesn't look in my direction once. I narrow my eyes at her back as she walks toward the line that still has at least three families in it with their children. I follow, but something feels off.

We make it on the ride and each grab one of the horses that rise and fall rhythmically. I'm being lulled to sleep when I notice that she is still looking around intently while the platform spins. Again, my eyes narrow and lock on hers as she tries to look beyond me at something she's noticed.

"Why are you looking at me that way?"

"What are you looking for? You have been acting weird for the past hour, looking at your watch every five minutes and bringing us back here to the merry-go-round." My voice raises just a little, as I don't want to make any of the little children uncomfortable. "You claim it's because you want to ride this thing, but you've spent the entire ride watching the perimeter. I feel like I'm in a damn thriller or spy novel."

She laughs a full belly laugh, and then she suddenly waves at someone or something behind me. I try to turn around, but we still haven't stopped moving, and I don't see anyone waving back.

"Relax. I'm not a spy, nor am I watching for a killer."

Neither her laughter, nor her playfulness appease me. She is up to something. I pull out my phone and open the camera.

"What are you doing, Kass?"

"Taking a picture of you." I click the shutter button three times. "I want to remember you in this moment, so I can accurately describe to mom and dad how you looked when I kill you."

She gasps and clasps her hand to her chest in feigned surprise. I'm still not laughing when the ride comes to a stop, and she hops off her horse. Yes, it's the high horse. No, the joke is not lost on me. No, I'm still not going to laugh. I wait a few seconds before I climb down and follow. Before I can make my way around toward the ride's exit, Lissa comes back into view.

"Come on, slowpoke. Asher's waiting for us."

A look of confusion passes over my face, until I scan the barricade and find a ginger beard on an angelic face. How had she known he was coming? How had he known to find us here? I will myself to keep walking, though I want to stop in my tracks and force her to tell me what in the hell is going on... between the two of them.

"Asher, so good to see you again," Lissa says in her most syrupy sweet voice, loud enough that I can hear her from 20 feet away. If it wasn't for the sound of the merry-go-round itself, half the damn crowd could've heard her. I don't hear his response, but I see him look up at me with a smile, and he takes a step forward. He must've read the confusion on my face because he stays where that one foot lands, his own brows furrowing. Malissa, on the other hand, is smiling from ear to ear, and my nostrils flare.

I compose myself as I come to stand in front of him. "Hello, Asher," I say with a smile that is genuine, and yet, I can tell by his face that he recognizes something is off.

"You don't quite look happy to see me here. I thought from your text that you would be happy I made it."

I hold up one finger, cutting him off, and pull my phone out of my pocket. "That's it." I say under my breath, though I can tell he's heard me because his brows drop in confusion again. He's super cute when he makes that face, but I can't focus on that right now. I open my text messages, and sure enough, there's a conversation between he and I that I did not participate in. I'm going to kill her, I say to myself, as I beg his forgiveness and lunge at my sister.

She takes off running with howls of laughter, and I run after her like a crazy woman half my age. Suddenly, I am stopped by a strong arm around my waist. I don't even fight, as I look down and recognize the arms I've dreamt about far too often in recent weeks wrapped around me.

"Whoa there." His breath is on my neck, and I melt into him. "I don't know what's going on, but I'm not going to let you do something you might regret shortly."

"It's okay. I took a picture of her on the merry-go-round, so our parents could have a recent, happy photo of her to use at the funeral."

He chuckles and pulls me tighter against his chest, the vibrations of his laugh working their way through my body. I sigh and wrap my hands around his arms, holding him in place. I have no idea where Malissa got off to, and I don't care. I have half a mind to leave her ass here.

CHAPTER 19
ASHER

I stand there holding her against me for what feels like both an hour and yet far too little time. When she grabs my arms, like she could hold me still, I nearly turn her around and kiss her. If not for the sounds of the fair creeping through the haze of lust, I might've done just that. Instead, I lean my head down near her ear again.

"Now, why did you want to kill your sister?" None of the possible reasons I've come up with prepare me for her answer.

"I wasn't the one who sent those texts."

I do turn her around then because I need to see her eyes. "What?"

She bites her lip, and my eyes lock onto that movement. "I was in the shower at the time of that conversation about meeting here at the fair."

I barely register the implication of her statement, as I picture her in the shower. I need to get it together. Here she is telling me that she was not the one I planned this outing with, and all I can focus on is how stiff my cock has gotten while holding her to me.

I grab her hand, and we walk toward the buildings along the perimeter of the festival. There is an empty bench, and I hope that if we sit and talk, the blood will once again return to my brain rather than my groin. I need some clarity...of thought and her feelings toward me.

"So, you're telling me it was your sister who invited me to meet you two here near the merry-go-round." Though I haven't asked it as a question, she still responds with an embarrassed nod.

"Does that mean you don't want me here?" My voice sounds weaker than I mean it to. I need to know the answer, but I don't want her thinking my heart depends on it. I'm not even sure what my heart wants. My body, on the other hand, I know exactly what it wants.

"No."

Her answer is so abrupt, I drop the hand I'm still holding.

"No, I didn't mean no."

She shakes her head, and I'm left dumbfounded that a woman who writes thousands of words every day can have such a hard time answering a simple question. She looks down at the ground, and I watch her back lift, as she takes three deep breaths. Finally, she turns her eyes back to mine and grabs my hand in both of hers.

"I'm sorry, that was all coming out so wrong." Her thumbs slowly caress the backs of my knuckles. "I am glad you're here. Really, I am. If you had come here because you had planned to all along, maybe for your love of funnel cakes, fine, but not because my sister is trying to play matchmaker." I watch the blush creep up into her cheeks before she looks down at the ground again. With my free hand, I lift her chin back to look at me. "I just don't want you to be here under false pretenses," she says quietly.

"If you are glad I'm here, then I'm glad your sister invited me."

"Really?" The squeak at the end of that one word makes me laugh so hard, I start coughing.

"It's not that funny." She releases my hands and pats me on the back.

"It most definitely was."

"So can I ask a favor?"

I raise my brow. There is something mischievous in the way her eyes sparkle.

"Since my sister thinks she's funny with her matchmaker antics, will you help me get her back?"

"Get her back how?"

"Pretend you are my boyfriend and that we were already dating before she came."

My grin is huge as I take her hand and pull her to stand with me. "How about we go find your sister and tell her she's forgiven." Her smile falls, and her lips purse in the sexiest possible way. I stare at her mouth and raise a brow. She licks her lips. I lean in close, and her breath hitches. "If you don't want me growling in public again, I suggest we go find your sister and enjoy this date." Her breaths are heavier now, but she nods in acquiescence. "Good."

***

The remainder of the day goes by far too fast as I enjoy my time with Kass and her sister. They're hilarious together. The banter never stops, and it reminds me why I constantly asked my parents for a sibling. I remember when Sarah was born, and Jesse finally had a sister. I wanted one so bad, and now I see why. Kass and Malissa know each other so well, even as adults.

I have enjoyed them so much that I'm slightly disappointed when Jesse shows up. We're still friends, and I'm always glad when we get to hang out, but I don't want anything or anyone to mess up the flow of the day like what has happened the last two times I got to spend time with Kass. I especially want no interruptions on the day I get to publicly hold her hand and playfully touch her as her fake boyfriend. Imagine my surprise when Jesse and Malissa hit it off and start walking together. He gives me a chance to spend time really getting to know Kass outside of her space, outside of the author I constantly interrupt.

We walk through the vendors hand-in-hand. In my other hand, I carry the items she purchases to add to her decor. She has a ceramic Dalmatian from a local sculptor and a photo print of the beautiful dogwoods down Main Street here. She's calling it her memories of the outing, and it is the cutest thing. She says she plans to put today's date with our names on it before she frames it for the wall.

"We can't leave without riding the ferris wheel," Malissa announces from behind us.

"Ugh." Kass' response both catches me off guard and makes me laugh.

"What's wrong?" I ask, pulling her in close.

"Kass isn't a fan. She's afraid of heights."

"It's not just the height. It's the fact that these machines are put together and taken apart so often, they cannot continue to be safe."

"Please, Kassie."

I want to support Kass' wish to stay on the ground, but something about getting her alone where she can't run has me adding my request to Malissa's. I even throw in a little pout, which garners a smile, and I know she's going to agree.

"Fine."

Malissa exhales a satisfied 'Yes' and pulls Jesse along toward the monstrous ride that is visible from a mile away. Kass is far less enthusiastic about getting to the ferris wheel. I see her looking up at the top carriage and then back at her sister while biting the inside of her lower lip. I've noticed that she does that when she's nervous. I lean in to whisper in her ear.

"I got you. You'll be safe with me."

She gives me a weak smile, and lets me lead her into the line. Malissa and Jesse are four groups ahead of us, which is good with me. They'll be far enough away to not hear what I have in mind.

This is one of the newer ferris wheels that have closed in carriages that just hang, allowing you a safe view from every direction.

"How many?" The carnie shouts, maybe a little louder than is needed.

"Two," I say, holding up two fingers.

"Ride alone or with another group of two?"

"She's already nervous, so alone, please."

The ride rolls itself around a full turn. Jesse and Malissa wave to us as they pass by.

"Couldn't you just take a picture from the top for me," Kass yells to her sister as they fly by. Malissa's laugh can be heard until they get halfway to the top.

Our carriage arrives, and we climb inside. Kass holds on so tightly to the walls of the carriage that her knuckles turn white. I sit directly across from her, so the car is balanced. I'll move once we make our first full rotation. I reach my hands out toward her, and she takes them in her own. They tremble slightly until we start moving, and then they become a vise around my fingers.

"Look at me, Kass. Focus on me."

She brings her eyes up to mine, and I smile. She doesn't reciprocate, still focused on the fear that has her frozen and her breathing shallow. We stop after our full rotation while the car behind us is loaded.

"See, we made it all the way around, and we're safe."

I lean to my left to look out over the side of the carriage door.

"No, what are you doing? Don't do that."

"What?"

"Don't lean out like that. The whole car moved when you moved."

"Did it?"

Though I hate that she is so afraid, and that Malissa made it seem like it was simple nerves, I need a way to get her over onto my side or for her to let me step over to her side. As much as she is already shaking, she would not make it through our top of the ride stops without a distraction.

"Yes. Please just sit still."

"The only one moving right now is you. You're shaking the car all over the place."

She looks around and then down at her legs, which are shaking. Her eyes go wide before she closes them tightly and takes a couple of deep breaths. I've watched her do the deep breath thing enough times now to realize she is trying to calm her nerves. Through all this, though, she never releases my hands.

"I can't believe I let you and Malissa talk me into this."

We start our next rotation, and I inwardly cringe at her accusation. We did talk her into this. The thought of getting her alone was my undoing. The sad part is that Malissa and Jesse were going to ride this contraption anyway, so I could have stolen a few moments down on the ground with her.

Her grip once again squeezes my fingers throughout the entire rotation, and when we stop with a lurch, she lets out a short squeal. I use the momentum of the car to pull her over onto my lap. Wrapping my arms around her, I pull her legs over mine, so her feet are on the seat next to me, and I hold her tight. It is all I can do to ignore the weight of her supple body on mine.

"The car's not balanced any more. It's not safe."

"Shh. Wrap your arms around my neck and breathe. You'll be fine. We're fine."

Surprisingly, she listens, and her hands reach around to my back as she buries her face into the curve of my neck. Her breath is warm, and I'm instantly regretting the position I'm holding her in when my cock twitches. There is no way to hide it from her should he become fully erect.

"Feel better," I ask when it's clear that her trembling has all but stopped. Her nearly imperceivable movements against my neck make my breath hitch slightly, and I curl my fingers into her legs, as I pull her in tighter. She gasps, and a smile spreads across my lips. This is exactly what I wanted, her relaxed and against me. When the ride starts its next rotation, she hardly moves.

"Did you fall asleep?"

She giggles and lifts her head to shake it from side to side.

"You smell good," she says, her voice low, before she lays her head back on my chest and inhales deeply at the spot where my neck and shoulder meet.

"Why, Ms. Gingham, I did not bring you over here, so you could take advantage of my good nature."

She giggles again, her hand reaching up to pull my head closer, so she can sniff up toward my ear. I lean in, giving her better access and growl when her breath touches my lobe.

"Sir, I thought we had an understanding about that growl of yours."

"Look around. Do you see any public?"

We had stopped again just two steps below the top. She hadn't even noticed the last two rotations. When she lifts her eyes and looks out, though, she jumps and tightens her hold on me, as if she would crawl into my skin if she could. A laugh rumbles in my chest, and she slaps at me playfully.

"It's not funny. I can't even see the buildings downtown."

"All you need to do is look at me."

She stays still for a few moments, and when she finally lifts her head, her eyes are still closed tight. It takes another few breaths before she opens them and looks into mine.

"There you are," I say with a smirk. "I was beginning to think you might never look at me again."

CHAPTER 20
KASSANDRA

From the moment Asher pulls me onto his lap, my entire system has been focused on the feel and smell of him. It is so hard not to run my tongue up his neck to see if his skin tasted as good as he smells. I know he pulled me to him as a distraction from my fear, but now there is nothing to distract me from his nearness. And then he tells me to look into his eyes with that sexy ass smirk of his, and my resolve comes undone.

I shift on his lap, trying to calm the ache between my thighs, and he moans, a low, guttural sound that immediately has my panties drenched. His eyes darken, and I bite my lip, my hands reaching up to cup his cheeks. He leans into them and shifts in his seat. His erection presses into my ass, and I barely hold in a moan of my own. Instead, I lean up and press my lips to his.

He opens his mouth, and I suck on his bottom lip. That is all it takes for his passion to flare. He grabs my ass and lifts me until I can put my legs on each side of him, straddling his hips. I lean down over him finally galvanized to run my tongue up his neck from the crux of his shoulder to his earlobe. He growls as I pull the tiny bit of flesh between my teeth. No sooner do I release it that he captures my mouth again, his tongue dancing with mine until we are both out of breath.

I pull back from his mouth, gasping in need for something more than air. His lips pull back in a look of satisfaction, as if he can read my thoughts. Maybe he can. My need must be written on my face. He lifts his hips, and his hardness rubs against the part of me screaming for his touch. I suck in air through my teeth, and then I feel the car stop again, but we never stop rocking. Leaning into him for stability, my eyes look out of the car's rails and freeze. There is nothing but sky in my view, no buildings or wires, nothing to break up the empty air. My chest tightens, and my eyes are like saucers.

"Stay with me, Kass."

His voice is soft, comforting. It's not enough this time. My heartbeat doubles, and my breaths come in rapid succession.

"Kassandra, look at me."

He is more assertive this time. I hear him, but I can't dampen the panic that has taken hold. He grabs my face and kisses me, trying to restore the distraction we had just moments ago been successfully enjoying. It's not enough.

"More," I eke out between shallow breaths.

He picks me up off him again, and a whimper leaves my lips. Whether it is from the loss of contact with his body or the greater feeling of insecurity, I can't say, but it soon becomes obvious he has a plan. With strength and quickness that should not have been possible with a woman my size, he twists me around, so that I am again sitting on his lap with my back to his chest.

"Grab my neck, Kassandra." His voice is forceful, and I comply. "Don't let go."

He kisses the back of my neck. His hands rub up from my hips to my stomach, bared by my raised arms. They continue making their way up until they find my breasts, cupping them through my bra. My breaths change from quick and shallow to long and deep. I begin to relax back into his chest and let my arms slip.

"I said keep them up around my neck," he barks, and I snap them back up with a gasp. As my head starts to clear from the panic, though my heart continues beating at an elevated rate, I let myself enjoy the feel of him kneading my breasts. My nipples respond to his attention, and he pinches them through the cotton cups. I wish I had thought to wear a sexier one with thinner materials.

He continues kissing my neck, which has always been a major turn on, and I want to feel his skin on mine. As if reading my mind again, his hands travel lower until he finds the band of my leggings. I expect him to push them down, and I wouldn't have stopped him, but he doesn't. I hold my breath for his next move, and he starts rocking his hips beneath my ass, his contained erection obvious against my bottom. He brings one hand back up to my nipple, sliding beneath the band of my bra, and he presses his other to my core through my pants while he continues grinding into me. I moan at the sensations of his hand rubbing up and down my covered slit.

"Already wet for me, baby?"

"Yes." My voice is shallow and breathless, my entire body on fire from his touch.

He stops his rubbing, and I want to complain, but his mouth is on my neck, his breath near my ear.

"Tell me what you want, Kassandra."

I can't think straight. My body is screaming for his hands, his mouth, his cock...anything. "Touch me." I grab his hands, and he says nothing about me having lowered my own from his neck, so I lead him where I need to be touched. When I slide our hands into my pants and under the waistband of my panties, he exhales a satisfied *mmmm*. When his fingers curl, pushing through to touch my swollen clit, my sharp inhale resounds above the noise of the ride.

"Shhhh. If someone hears you, I'll have to stop. You don't want that, do you?"

He applies more pressure, the pads of his fingers circling my clit while his other hand squeezes my breasts, first one and then the other pinching each nipple in succession. I lean my head back on his chest and put my hands back around his neck. I turn my face toward his, and his lips find mine, capturing a moan I'm unable to control.

"Asher." His name is a whisper, as I feel my walls begin to clench, my release imminent.

He kisses up my jaw line until his mouth is in line with my ear. "Come for me."

His movements are methodical, never changing pace or losing pressure. He brings me to the breaking point, and I shatter in his hands. When I can no longer contain myself, he releases my breast and covers my mouth while I ride the waves. He holds me there until my writhing stops and my breaths calm. If his arms weren't around me, I would have puddled on the floor of the car like jelly.

He pulls his hand from my pants and slides his fingers into his mouth. His eyes close as he sucks my juices from them. Somehow, that action is more erotic than him having made me come in public. I sit there transfixed, while he licks between his fingers, as if he were cleaning the most delicious cake batter from a beater.

"One more time around, and we get off this ride. Are you okay?"

I don't trust myself to say anything yet, so I just nod and try to steady myself enough to leave his lap and sit on the seat next to him. I instantly miss his body against mine, but I focus on keeping my face neutral.

The men walk us to my car, Asher never releasing my hand, and I can't wipe the smile off my face.

"You enjoyed the ride that much?" Malissa asks, her inflection exaggerated.

From the corner of my eye, I see Asher put his fist to his mouth and cough, as if trying to stifle a laugh. I glare at him sideways, but the glint in his eye has me laughing too.

"What's so funny?" she asks. "I thought for sure you would be in a full-blown state of panic by the time we got off there."

"You know, sis, it's kind of fucked up that you were hoping for me to be miserable on the ride."

She looks askance, and her lip quivers slightly.

"Actually," Jesse interjects, "she spent most of the ride worried about you. I would almost say she felt guilty for pushing you into it."

I soften my stare at her. I'm not mad. In fact, I'm feeling entirely too good to be mad at anything.

"I am glad you made it through okay," Malissa says, blinking back tears. I let go of Asher's hand and reach to put my arm around her.

"I'm not upset. I am, however, glad I went with Asher and not with you. Sounds like your ride was miserable." I bump her with my shoulder.

"It wasn't as bad as he makes it sound, but I was worried about you."

"I survived, thought it was..." I pause for a second with a glance toward Asher. "Touch and go a few times." He turns his face away, and I see his lips curling up from the side.

When we get to the car, we realize that the guys had not parked too far from us. Maybe it was a sign or likely just a strange coincidence, but considering Asher had never seen my car, and Jesse didn't know he was here, I'm leaning toward divine providence. That's what a good mood, and an amazing orgasm will do for you.

"Hey, Ash, man, what's that on your tire?"

"What do you mean?"

We all look down the sidewalk a couple cars, and, sure enough, there is something gray lying across his tire. He walks off a few feet toward his truck, angling himself for a better view.

"Hang on," he says before he picks up the pace. We all watch him reach his hand out gingerly toward what looks like a piece of gray cloth. After a few moments, he reaches in with his other hand and pulls out...

"Is that a kitten?" Malissa's yell accompanies an excited squeak. While her outburst may have been a question, his approach leaves no question that he is, indeed, holding a tiny gray kitten. "Oh my goodness, it's so small. The poor thing."

"What are you going to do with that, man?" Jesse asked.

"Duh, he's going to take care of it." Malissa elbowed him in a playful way that belied the fact they had just met a couple hours ago. I might've thought it cute if I wasn't fixated on the furry ball in Asher's big hands.

"What are you going to do with it?" I ask.

"I don't know," he says, his voice unsure, and his face a mask of confusion.

"Well, we can't just leave it here, or it'll end up in someone else's tire well, and they might not notice it," I say in agreement with Malissa, but I can tell he's still not sure what to do with this kitten. "Have you ever taken care of a kitten before?" I ask, and he shakes his head no.

"We had dogs when I was younger," he replies. "My grandmother didn't like cats. She thought they were the devil." I laugh.

"He's serious," Jesse says. "There are lots of people around here who think cats are bad omens, and not just the black ones."

"And what about you," Malissa asks, finger pointed at his chest.

"I think they're just like any other animal. They want to live, love, and be taken care of. That's all any of us really want."

"Look at you, waxing poetic," Asher quips.

Jesse shrugs. "Joke all you want. I'm not the one stuck with a kitten."

As Asher holds the ball of fluff, it stretches and then curls into itself in his hands, and I see his face soften.

"How about I take it," I offer. "I had a kitten when I was younger, so I have some experience. And, I'm home all day. You can come check on it whenever you deliver the mail." He looks at me with those uncertain eyes again, and my heart melts.

"Are you sure?" He searches my face for any uncertainty I might have. "That's a lot of responsibility, and a lot of interruptions to your writing."

"You're a writer?" Jesse asks. "That's cool. My sister wanted to be a writer, but my parents told her it was a dumb idea."

I look at him and purse my lips. "Let me guess," I say, mimicking voices I've heard, "That's not a job. You won't make any money." I try to hold back the venom. While my parents are supportive, not everyone in the family has been, and Charles certainly wasn't.

"Well," Malissa interjects, "Everyone who says that is just wrong. My sister is proof of how wrong they are. She is highly successful and owns a huge house from the money she makes."

"I'll have to tell her...my sister, that is. There's no telling my parents anything." He and Asher both laugh.

"Lissa, do you think you could follow us to the house in my car? I'll go with Asher and hold the kitten. We will have to stop on the way and get some things for it."

Jesse puts his hands in the pockets of his jeans. "I'm gonna have to head home," he says, "to go help take care of our animals."

"You have animals?" Malissa asks, no longer interested in the tiny kitten that is now curled up at my chest.

"Jesse's family owns a farm."

"And I help out in the evenings when I'm not at work. My parents aren't getting any younger."

"That's nice of you," she says, looking up at him. "It was very nice to meet you."

He takes her offered hand and then leans in to kiss her on the cheek. "Likewise." He turns to walk away and then seems to remember that we're standing here. "It was nice to meet you too, Kass. And Asher, I'll check with you later."

"Yeah, man, we'll hang out soon," Asher responds.

Jesse takes off across the street and climbs into his truck. Malissa watches until he pulls away, and we can no longer see his taillights.

Once we're situated in the truck, and the kitten is asleep on my lap, I watch the man behind the wheel. It's been a long time since I've found myself looking at a man that I genuinely like. Of course, he is attractive, but he is also genuinely kind and lacking pretense. The fact that he had considered taking care of this kitten without any idea how just proves his kindness. Hell, the fact that he took care of me on the ferris wheel without asking anything in return says as much. I shudder as emotions threaten to overtake me.

"Are you cold?" He asks.

"Maybe a little."

It isn't completely a lie. After feeling his warmth for so long stuck in that ferris wheel carriage in the air, I am a little chilly.

"Thank you for offering to take care of the kitten. I really had no idea what I was going to do."

"I'm sure you would've figured it out. You seem to think well on your feet. Besides," I say with a shrug, "It's the least I can do to repay you."

I can only see his face in profile, and I can tell his brow is furrowed. "Repay me for what?"

"For this weekend. For agreeing to pretend to be my boyfriend." I cringe. "I can't believe I'm even saying that. Forty-five years old talking about a boyfriend just so my sister won't feel the need to play matchmaker...or worse, try and talk me into getting back with my ex." I shake my head and wrinkle my nose at that thought. "You didn't have to agree to any of that, but you did, and I appreciate it. I appreciate you..." I look down at the sleeping kitten, "and your distractions."

He chuckles. "About that..." He looks toward me, and our eyes meet.

"That," I say, "was just icing on the cake."

He smiles, and we fall into a comfortable silence.

CHAPTER 21
KASSANDRA

S har woke in a strange bed. It took a moment to orient herself and remember the night before. She groaned. "What the hell was I thinking?" she asked aloud to what she thought was an empty room. A familiar voice answered back from a chair in the far corner.

"I was wondering the same thing myself," he said.

"I don't need your judgment this morning. I have enough of my own."

She sat up in the middle of the bed. Her hair was a disheveled mess. She could see herself in the mirrored doors to what she could only assume was a closet. Geez, she thought, reaching up to pull the pins from her hair and let down what small bits were left in the bun she had coiled at the back of her head last night before leaving her hotel room. It felt like days had passed rather than...

"What time is it?" She asked the figure in the corner.

"Just about noon."

She flopped back on the bed. He chuckled in that low, sultry way of his, and she felt a stirring between her thighs.

"Is that all you're gonna do? Sit over there in the shadows and laugh at me?"

There was no bite to her words. She knew she deserved it. Okay, she didn't deserve what had happened, but considering he of all people had been the one to step in and save her, she could afford him a few giggles at her expense.

"No, that was not all I had planned for today. In fact, I had plenty of other things planned for the day besides babysitting you."

That statement riled her. "I don't need a babysitter, okay. I am grown, and even grown folk make bad decisions sometimes."

She sat up again when she heard him stand. She wasn't just going to lay there and take whatever he had to say.

"How many bad decisions have you made this week, pretty?"

Her breath caught in her throat as he stood in front of her. Not only was he shirtless, but his loose pajama bottoms also hung so low on his hips, he might as well have been naked. She salivated at the thought of once again tasting what was barely hidden beneath that waistband. She cleared her throat and looked up at him. He was watching her the way he did when he expected a response and was waiting for her to comply.

"Why don't you tell me?" she said defiantly. "You think you have all the answers."

"Let's see." He put his hands on the bed, so that he was eye-level with her. "You invited a stranger to your room and stripped naked. You didn't even know his name, nor did you ever ask. You simply let him fuck you senseless and leave without a word."

She swallowed, as he put a knee on the bed.

"For the next few days, you stalked the beach, watching for him, and when you finally saw him, the man you had been thinking about for days, you did nothing even when he told you to go after what you wanted. You just sat there."

She took in a shuddering breath and looked down at her hands.

"Look at me."

Though his voice remained calm, he might as well have

yelled the way her eyes snapped back up to his. He put another knee on the bed.

"Then, you decided to join up with a frat boy and bar hop with him until he was pissy drunk. Did you leave when you had the opportunity?"

He stalked toward her, one hand and knee moving at a time. She bit her lip. If she had been alone, even if he had been saying this on the phone, tears would have run from her eyes at the truth of it and how much danger she had put herself in. Instead, in his presence, in his overwhelming closeness, shivers of desire ran through her. He moved until his face was directly in front of hers.

"Now, you wake up in that same stranger's bed disoriented, and you don't try to leave. Why?"

His breath was a whisper on her lips, and his eyes bore into hers.

"I'm not afraid of you," she said.

"Maybe you should be."

He captured her mouth, pushing her back onto the bed and covering her body with his own. His hands, mouth, and tongue were everywhere at once, it seemed, and her body ignited. A moan slipped, and she wasn't sure if it was hers or his. Maybe it came from both of them. He slid her barely-there dress straps off her shoulders and sucked her nipple into his mouth. His teeth grazed the sensitive tip until her back arched. He repeated the actions with the other nipple before kissing his way down her stomach. Her hips lifted off the bed in anticipation as he settled himself between her legs.

He inhaled deeply, nose nearly pressed against her slit. She watched his eyes roll back in ecstasy, as if he was seated before the most delicious meal. He looked up into her eyes and slid his tongue between her lips, lightly caressing the tip of her clit. She clenched the sheets on either side and tried to lift her hips to increase the pressure of his flitting tongue, but his hands held her in place. He continued to tease her, tongue finding her hole and lapping all the way back to her clit before circling the bud faster while finally increasing the intensity of his ministrations.

The pressure inside her increased to match him, and she threw her head back, no longer able to hold herself upright. Her moans came more frequently, as she got closer to her release. When his lips grabbed onto her clit and sucked, her head snapped back to watch him.

"Don't stop." She was so close. "Oh my god!"

Just as she thought it was all over for her and that her body would shatter into a thousand pieces, he lifted his head and smiled.

"Not yet, pretty."

"What?" Her question was breathy.

He licked right below her belly button, and then pulled his tongue slowly back up to her sternum. He worked his way up her body until she felt his cock, hard and ready, between her legs. She moaned. He situated his face right above hers as she lifted her hips to better accommodate him.

"My name is Mack, and when you come, it'll be my name on your lips."

He slid into her effortlessly, filling her at the same time his tongue entered her mouth. She tasted her own tanginess on his lips, and it only added to her arousal. Her hands wrapped around his back until she slid them down to grasp his ass, trying to pull him as far into her as possible. Without missing a stroke, he grabbed her hands and held them above her head, directing her to hold onto the headboard.

She moaned as he picked up the pace, her ankles propped on his shoulders. She used the leverage of the headboard and his body to lift herself off the bed until he hit the angle that took her breath away.

"Fuuuuck."

"That's it, pretty. Take this cock. Shit."

She matched him stroke for stroke, pulling her hips up until they were both breathing heavy. Her walls tightened around him as she raced toward her release.

"Shit, I'm gonna come."

Her toes curled, as her body went rigid. Still, he pounded in and out of her, ensuring every inch of her walls pulsed around every inch of him.

"Yes, yes, yes."

He released one of her hips and slid his hand up toward her throat. His breathing was ragged with the exertion and control, as he held off his own orgasm to elongate hers. Their eyes locked, and with nostrils flaring, he commanded.

"Say my name."

She stared at him, her hands still locked around the top of the headboard. She wanted to defy him, to deny the power he had over her body. When he squeezed his hand at the base of her neck, though, she could deny him no longer.

Between shallow breaths, almost inaudibly, "Mack" left her lips, and she fell apart. Her hands left the headboard to lie at her sides, and her body became putty in his hands. No sooner had she spoken than his own erratic breaths matched his thrusts. He arched his back and yelled his release. Her own body had relaxed enough that she felt every throb of his cock, and she smiled before exhaustion took her.

I yawn and look at the time on my phone. Normally, sex scenes flow easily, but this one took forever, and it is already late. Granted, I hadn't sat down at my desk until mid-afternoon, after Lissa left for home. Something moves from the corner of my eye, and I see my new friend, Ferris, stretching from his warm bed on the far corner of my desk. I will likely regret the decision to let him sleep there when he gets bigger, but he's just too cute to let him get too far away.

Ferris looks toward the floor from the desk and then at me. His small mewl of frustration is more of a squeak. "Soon, my little friend, you will be jumping everywhere." I pick him up and nuzzle him to my cheek for a moment before putting him on the floor in front of his food. Now that he is awake, I will not get much sleep. Litter training a feral kitten, even one this young, is exhausting. "But I love you already."

I think of Asher, and a smile crosses my lips. I grab my phone and snap a picture.

> Ferris is wondering if you will be coming to see him tomorrow.

> Asher: Ferris?

> Photo sent

> Asher: You named him Ferris?

> Yes. You found him on your wheel after we had been on the ferris wheel, so his name is Ferris. It suits him. He runs around like crazy, stops for a few seconds to eat, and then wanders about until he gets stuck somewhere for a nap.

> Asher: LOL. You're not regretting taking him, are you?

> Absolutely not! He slept on my chest last night and still didn't hog the covers.

> Asher: zip-lipped emoji

LOL. Goodnight.

Asher: Night.

CHAPTER 22
ASHER

She named the fucking cat Ferris after the ferris wheel ride. I'm still feeling the effects of getting no sleep last night because I kept hearing her moans like a siren song, and now she tells me this. My cock jumps to attention as soon as I read the word ferris. This woman is going to be the death of me. Death by erection. If it's not already a thing, it will be.

I replay the entire weekend. Her apology for sending me away when her sister arrived. Our kiss outside the steakhouse. Her asking me to pretend to be her boyfriend. The feel of her soft body curled up on my lap. My god, she felt so good. She tasted so good. Not for the first time today, my hand slides to my cock trying to tamp down the desire I can't act on. I want this woman something terrible, and now we have a cat together.

How do I go by there daily and not kiss her lips, not grab her hips, not hear her cry out? These questions have been plaguing me since I dropped her off last night. I want to text her back and ask her if we can prolong this boyfriend-girlfriend thing a little longer, so I can show her the benefits. Oh, who am I kidding, I just want her. I want to run my hands over every curve and trace my tongue over every dimple. I want to fall asleep with my head comfortably cradled by those pillowy thighs. Propriety be damned, I will find a way to have her.

The workday is dragging. Mondays usually suck, at least until people start coming in after work, but the fact I've put off morning deliveries just makes the day feel even longer. More than once, Louise asks me why I'm hanging around and not out making deliveries. Somehow, I don't think that the response 'my crush is your favorite author, and she's asked me to come by in the afternoons' will be acceptable. I simply make some kind of noncommittal response about waiting for the early afternoon drop-offs to finalize my delivery route.

My thoughts, however, run far from drop-offs and deliveries. They run to where I want to end my day and my night. They don't, however, run with any good answers on how to make that second one happen. I still have not figured out what it is about Kassandra that pulls at me, but I also feel inadequate to pursue her fully. Not only is she one of the most beautiful women I've ever met, but she's also intelligent, ambitious, driven, and kind. She's older, has obviously been through some difficult times, yet she's not jaded like Louise and Gabby. She's still playful, and there's a certain vulnerability that she tries to keep hidden. How can I even consider myself on her level?

I'm none of those things. I might have been many years ago, but I've grown soft, complacent. Though I finished my degree in architectural engineering with honors before returning home, I've not used it once. I should have made so many upgrades to the house by now, but I've not done anything. Instead, I spend my days in this uniform and my evenings in front of the TV watching home improvement shows. I should be on one of those shows, not just admiring their handiwork. I could be doing so much more. Why would a woman like Kassandra, who is living her dream, want a man like me who seems to have forgotten he once had dreams?

"You're moping again, McNeil." Louise makes her way through the labyrinth of mail carts I have strewn about the back room, as I prepare the afternoon delivery route. "Something happen between you and that woman from the steakhouse?"

She starts sorting some of the smaller packages into their carts before she stops to look at me. My lips form a tight line as I wait for the impending what, I don't know. I just know I'm not going to like it from the look on her face.

"Oh, maybe the problem is that nothing has happened. From the way you two looked at each other, and then all the time you spent outside, I thought for sure..." She trails off, waiting expectantly for me to fill in the blank.

"What is your point, Louise?"

"My point is, you're a damn sad sack today, and you're bringing me down. I have Gabby for that and don't need you adding to it."

I blink at her multiple times. What is she saying? Is she telling me to leave?

"You're a great guy, Asher McNeil. You're too good to be stuck around here, but I enjoy your positive energy, so I don't push. I don't know anything about that woman up there, but I do know I saw a spark in you when she waved across the restaurant that I haven't seen in years. Shoot your shot. If not with her, then at least with life. Don't be like me."

"Louise, I..."

"Don't tell me. Tell her. Tell yourself. Do something about it, whatever it is. Something has you dreaming about more than this post office and that house you grew up in. Take advantage of that spark and do something."

127

I nod. I don't know what else to do. I don't know what to say. I gather up the last of my deliveries and write down the route, so I don't miss anything. Before I walk out the door, I do something I would never have imagined doing. I turn around and hug Louise, crushing her arms to her sides, as she sputters in surprise. I kiss her cheek and mutter a quick 'thank you' before leaving out the back and climbing into my Bronco.

It is later than I expected when I park my truck outside of Kassandra's house. The first thing I notice is the new poles up around the clearing and gravel lot out front. She really did add more lights out here I think to myself with a smile. Though she had seemed genuinely concerned for my safety that night we came back late from the steakhouse, I thought she had forgotten her plan when it was still dark out here after the festival.

Hopefully, I'm not showing up at an inopportune time. It's still too bright outside for me to judge what room she might be in. I'd hate for her to be at her desk writing, but I promised I would come check on Ferris. I grab her packages from the front seat where I had placed them before leaving the office. Everyone else's went into bins in the back, but hers rode along with me. If she reads all the books I bring her weekly, I don't know how she finds the time to write.

My foot hits the first step to the porch when my phone buzzes in my back pocket. I readjust the pouches in my hands to grab it.

> Kassandra: Hey, can you come around to the back. I can't come answer the door at this moment, but the patio doors are unlocked.

I nearly fall on my ass off the steps in shock. How did she know it was me? More than that, she trusts me to let myself in. My smile grows, as I make my way around the house and through the gate. I stop in my tracks when I get through the hedges that encircle the inner patio area. It's an absolute oasis back here. The kidney-shaped pool is huge and sparklingly clean. There is a hot tub and a pool house. There is also a well-tended garden area toward the forest's edge with benches. The patio itself borders the pool, and there are four lounge chairs along the length on both sides. This is my dream brought to life, and I take a moment to just enjoy the view. There's no excuse for why I haven't built this for myself, even if it were outside of my grandparents' house.

When my phone vibrates again, I realize I have been standing here too long, and I make my way up onto the lanai. I could have spent the rest of the evening taking in the design and details here as well, but I don't want her worrying. The glass door slides silently, and I take in the great room that is now in shadows from the trees hiding the sun.

"Good evening, Asher."

Her voice is both clear and loud, as if she's right next to me, but when I look around, I see no one. I give a quiet greeting in return. When she says nothing more, I put the mailers on the counter where she has had me drop other packages. I still don't hear her move or see her anywhere. Turning around, I jump at the unexpected figure in one of the recliners. She pulls her lips tightly together as the edges curl while I try to calm my heartbeat.

CHAPTER 23
KASSANDRA

I nearly piss myself trying to hold in my laugh at his screech. I might've fallen out of the chair completely if Ferris hadn't been asleep on my chest. As it is, the kitten stirred slightly when I said hello in the first place. I don't want to disturb him too much.

"It's not funny."

"Oh, it's hilarious."

"You didn't think it was so funny when you got scared." He raises both eyebrows, and memories of his hands all over me flood through my mind.

"No, but you were very kind to take care of me."

"It was my pleasure, Kass."

He leaned back against the counter watching me, and a warmth spread through my core. His pleasure the other night was my pleasure. The erotic vision he presented licking my juices from his fingers fill my mind. Thank goodness for this kitten holding me in place. I needed to change the direction of this conversation.

"Did you have many deliveries to make today?"

"Enough," he responded tersely.

I have never been very good at hiding my thoughts or

emotions. The confusion I felt at his one-word answer must have shown on my face because he expanded on his response.

"They were spread all over town. We may be rural, but that simply means we're more spread out. You had the most individual packages, though, as usual."

"Oh really?"

"Yes. You must have been book shopping again because they are all poly mailers."

"Do you know everyone's purchase history, Asher?"

I idly rub the kitten's curled back while Asher watches me. I feel the heat in his eyes, and I wish I knew how to flirt. I wish I were closer to his age, or even younger, so I could feel comfortable flirting with him. Oh, who am I kidding, I wouldn't have felt comfortable flirting with him even if I was younger. I've never flirted, simply followed along with what the guy I was interested in wanted. From the look on Asher's face while he watched Ferris sleep on my chest, I wanted to follow along with his thoughts.

"No, but I don't usually spend extended periods of time with the townsfolk because I've known most of them my whole life. And none of them make great fake girlfriends."

I laugh, a full laugh, and Ferris lifts his head.

"Sorry, kitten." He looks at me and mewls. "Ok, time to get up."

Asher raises a brow in question. He probably thinks I'm crazy for talking to the cat, but how else would you communicate with one. I simply shrug and carry the ball of fur around the counter to his food and water dishes. I hear Asher move and turn to catch him looking at my ass through my t-shirt dress when I bend over to put Ferris on the floor.

"So, what do you look for in a great fake girlfriend?" I ask quietly, trying to appear nonchalant about his comment.

"Hmm? Oh..." He laughs to himself, and I stand up straight to look him in the eye. Well, as close to in his eye as I can get being at least six inches shorter than him and on the other side of the large island. I put my hands on my hips. He, however, is not buying my feigned impatience, his tilted grin and raised brows calling my bluff.

He looks down at Ferris, who is now asleep again with his head on his food dish, and stalks toward me. My heart rate increases, and sweat beads on the back of my neck. His pupils are dilated to the point they almost look black in the shadowed kitchen. I take a step back and am stopped by the pantry door. He is now standing so close; I have to look up. I swallow, about to say something, but he beats me to it.

"What do I want in a fake girlfriend?"

He draws out the word 'fake' until it is like a song. I nod, though I barely move, still captivated by his dark gaze. He reaches out his left hand and tucks an unruly strand of hair behind my ear. His right hand strokes down my arm before settling on my waist. He uses that hand to pull me into him, his left hand grasped in my hair. I feel his breath along my ear and shudder, my eyes fluttering closed at the sensation.

"I want her soft and pliable in my hands." His hand leaves my waist to grab my ass and force our bodies to mold together. "I want her to crave my touch until she is breathless." He pulls tighter on my hair, and my breath hitches. His voice gets huskier with each statement, and I am ready to be a puddle on the floor. "I want her to scream my name every time she comes." Holy hell, my pussy twitches at his words, and I lift on my toes trying to press my thighs together.

"Asher?"

"Yes, Kassandra."

His voice is gravely, and a small moan leaves my lips. His grip tightens to a degree that should be painful, but the only ache is the one between my thighs. I want to be the fake girlfriend he just described. He nuzzles his nose into my ear and then runs it down my neck. I'm losing my wits quickly. Clearing my throat, I ask, "Would you like to go for a swim?"

His eyebrows nearly raise off his face. His sly laugh tells me that I'm still not fooling him with my attempted distractions.

"You know, I didn't come prepared for a swim, so all I have to wear are my boxers."

I close my eyes for a second at the image my mind conjures. When I open them again, he is staring at me intently. I need to ask him something serious, but I can hardly think straight with his body against mine. A swim will at least let me get out of his arms for a few minutes.

"I'm ok with it if you are."

His eyes sparkle, and he nods.

"Will the fuzzy one be okay in here alone?"

I look down at Ferris who is still balled up in the food plate.

"He'll be fine if we don't stay out there all night. I'd just like to stretch my muscles before it's completely dark out, and the furball fell asleep on me before I could go."

Though he finally releases me to head toward the back door, that heated look of his returns. It takes a moment to register what I've said to get him going. Heat rises into my cheeks, and I walk in the opposite direction.

"I'll be right out. I'm gonna grab us a couple of towels."

We leave the patio door cracked in case Ferris wakes up. He may not find his way outside, but maybe if he cries, one of us will hear him. Asher is already in the pool, having left his clothes folded on one of the lounge chairs closest to the lanai.

"I was thinking," Asher says from the middle of the pool.

"Wow, you move quickly."

"I nearly jumped in the pool before I came in the house earlier. You have a gorgeous patio." He swims to the side of the patio and looks up at me expectantly.

"Thank you," I say with a laugh. "It was definitely the selling point for the house, along with the great view from my desk."

"I think you should contact the library and offer to do a book signing," he blurts with a nervous grin.

"What?" I stand frozen with the towels in my hand.

He shakes his head. "Never mind. Are you coming in?" He waves toward the pool steps, gesturing for me to get in the water.

Pushing aside the question that still has me stunned, I place the towels on the edge of the pool near the ladder, so we can grab them easily when we're ready to get out. The temperature is perfect for an early evening swim, but sometimes the wind whips around the house, and it's enough to make your nipples pucker. I pull my dress over my head and lay it on the chaise near his clothes. I had double checked that my bikini was still tied when I went to the laundry room. No one else has ever been here during my swims, so I don't have any suits with more coverage, and I didn't want a wardrobe malfunction. Thankfully, I've never been self-conscious of my body, cellulite and all. Asher inhales sharply, and I know he isn't bothered by my size either.

"That is a great color on you."

I look down at the bright yellow bikini top holding in my 38DD's and smile. It does look good against my tanned skin. Another reason I like to write in the morning is so I can spend the afternoon at the pool. This place has become my sanctuary, and I'm somewhat surprised at how little I mind his intrusion on it. I should be more bothered, but looking at the water rivulets running off his bald head and down his bare torso has me as unbothered as possible.

"Are you getting in, or are you just going to stare at me?"

I'm still reeling somewhat from his earlier suggestion of a live author signing. Could I put myself out there like that? I shrug and then realize he might take that as a response to his question, so I add a 'Maybe I'm just going to enjoy the view' aloud.

"Suit yourself, beautiful."

He glides onto his back, smoothly transitioning into a backstroke across the pool. I'm going to join him, but for now, I can't take my eyes off how graceful and fluid his movements are. It reminds me of how easily his hands glided over my body the other night, fluidly guiding me toward one of the most amazing orgasms I've had in a long time. My body heats at the memory, and I slowly move toward the edge of the pool, not taking my eyes off him. When his eyes open to find me at the stairs, I gasp at the intensity of his stare. I'm not going to make it through this night untouched.

CHAPTER 24
ASHER

The air hangs stagnant when I look up and she's no longer watching me from the lounge chairs. I look around frantically, hoping she didn't get cold feet and run back in the house. Then I find her taking the first step into the pool. She is an absolute vision with her beautiful hair piled atop her head, and that damn bikini hiding nothing from view. I did not expect her to be beautifully tanned everywhere, and I wonder if she has tan lines beneath those impossibly small bits of cloth. I can't see not one line from where I'm watching, and the idea of her swimming naked has my cock at attention.

I'm glad I'm already in the water, else she'd get a full show of my interest. As it is, I home in on her lush body and make my way across the pool. Whatever does or doesn't happen tonight, I need to get my hands on that skin. I want to touch every curve. Hell, I want to lick every dimple. From the little taste of her release I got on the ferris wheel, I could gladly lose myself between those thighs. She finally latches on to my gaze, and her gasp makes my balls tighten. I want to ask her what she likes, but I'm afraid she'll get that fearful look in her eyes and run like she almost did when I mentioned signing her books at the library.

I stop at the bottom the stairs and hold out my hand to her. It takes a few seconds before she accepts it and steps down into the pool fully.

"You look like you belong in the water."

A heartbeat later, she says, "I was thinking the same about you, gliding through the water like you were born in it."

"Yes," I say, twirling her around in front of me, "but I don't look like this."

Her blush is like an aphrodisiac. Here in the water, with her wearing that damn bikini, my libido is even more active than it was in the house. I pull her into me, and her slick skin slides against mine in a most seductive way. I doubt she realizes how damn sexy she is.

"You make me crazy. Did you know that?"

"I haven't done anything."

She is breathless, and I'm losing the fight over my control. I hate this fake dating idea. It was cute at the festival, but then that damn ride. Shit, I want her to be mine for real.

"That's the thing," I say, cupping her cheek. "You don't have to do anything. From the moment you walked out of your door and smiled at me, I've been crazed. That little peek of those amazing breasts you tried to cover with your robe, and them thick thighs in front of my face were enough to have me standing at attention."

She tries looking down, but I hold her cheek in place. This attraction, this tension between us, is a little more than I can take. I need to know how she feels, if she actually wants me too. She raises her eyes back to mine, and there is resolve in them. She bites her lip, and I want her to bite mine. I continue to back further into the deep end. Though I know she can swim, I want her holding onto me. Her voice is breathy when she finally speaks again.

"I couldn't stop thinking about you the rest of that day. Your beautiful smile, gray eyes, and perfectly formed calves. They kept me distracted for three days. I couldn't even write my story because every time I thought about my male main character, it was your face I saw."

My heart leaps in my chest, and I hug her to me. She threads her arms around my neck and her legs wrap around my waist. The press of her heat against my stomach even in the refreshing water, has my cock ready to rip through both of our underwear. It takes me a couple of deep breaths before I can focus my thoughts enough to not strip her naked and plow into her. It has been years since I've been so consumed by a woman.

I kiss her temple and then work my way to her earlobe before licking down her neck. Her sigh is like a purr against my ear. I kiss and suck on the delicate skin. As much as I want to make her mine, I try my best not to mark her. I have no claim to her body or her heart.

"Asher." I pretend that I do not hear her whisper. I don't want this moment to end. "Asher." This time, her voice is a little louder, more direct. I kiss her jawline one more time before lifting my eyes to find hers. Her eyes are hooded, pupils dilated. Damn. Is that desire in her gaze? I open my mouth to say her name back, and she kisses me. It is the softest, sweetest, most tentative kiss I've ever felt, but her initiating is such a turn on that I deepen it. One, or perhaps both of us moan, as our tongues meet.

Her legs tighten around my waist. She grinds her heat against me, and I growl against her mouth. My hands reach around and cup her ass beneath her bikini bottoms. She gasps and grinds even harder. I spread her cheeks with my hands, sliding my fingers along from her asshole to her clit.

"Please." She buries her face in the indent between my neck and shoulder, gently nipping at my skin.

"Please what, Kass? Tell me what you want."

She lifts her head and says, "Touch me. Make me come."

It takes all my control not to smile and comply, but I have something else in mind.

"Not yet, beautiful. I want something more, something I've been dreaming about."

I walk us back to the side of the pool where the water is a little shallower. I see where she left the towels, and I get a glorious idea. With one hand rubbing her ass and along her slit, I slide the other hand up her back while recapturing her mouth. I lightly tug on the strings tied around her back, and they fall loose. Trailing my hand up further, I untie the strings around her neck as well. Knowing that she is holding herself up with her legs, I pull both hands around to the front of her body and remove her top, discarding it onto the patio next to the pool.

Her nipples tighten as soon as my hands find her breasts, and her breath hitches. They are perfectly weighted, hefty in all the right ways. And her dark areolas have me salivating knowing I won't even be able to fit them in my mouth. I dip my head for a taste, tracing the roundness with my tongue, circling inward until I pull the tight tip between my teeth. She hisses and pulls my head in tighter against her. I repeat the process with the other breast, and her breathing goes ragged. Good.

Pushing her up against the pool wall, I capture her lips again while also unfolding one of the towels on the edge of the patio. My hands run down her sides until I can grab her gloriously thick thighs. When I untangle her legs from my waist, she whines against my mouth.

"Don't worry, beautiful, I'll make it all better in a second."

She pulls her lips from mine and looks at me curiously. I smirk and capture her breast in my mouth again, tugging on the nipple until she is panting. I slowly untie her bikini bottoms while I continue to enjoy the feel and taste of her skin. Trailing my lips up her chest and neck, I lean in close to her ear.

"I need to taste you."

Before a gasp can even leave her lips, I lift her onto the patio atop the towel I'd unfolded. With her hips poised precariously on the edge of the pool, I slide my arms under her legs and placed them on my shoulders. She stares down at me wide-eyed. I hold her gaze for a moment before looking down at the delicious buffet before me. She is so soft in all the right ways, and I lean close to breath her in.

"Damn, you smell so good."

I rub my nose up and down her slit, listening to the changes in her breaths. I am going to enjoy every second of this.

"I've been unable to sleep thinking of how good you taste, and I barely got to tap the well with my fingers."

I wrap my hands around her thighs and spread her lips apart.

"I want you to come all over my face, Kassandra. I want to lick up every drop."

Her head drops back onto the towel, and I plunge my tongue into her pussy. I work it around the edge of her hole before licking up to her clit. It is already engorged and waiting for attention. The moment my tongue flicks over the sensitive bud, Kassandra lets out the most satisfying moan that makes my balls tighten. I latch onto her clit and suck until she grabs my head, pushing it into her. I will gladly die like this. When she releases me again, I stretch my hands up toward her breasts to find she is already pinching her own nipples. I look up to watch, and she is staring at me.

"Fuck, you're so damn sexy."

She cups my cheek, though my mouth is once again buried between her lips. Needing to please her, I attack her pussy like a starving man, licking and sucking until she is writhing. I can't get enough of her feel, her taste, the sound of her moans. When she slides her hand over my head again, I slip two fingers inside her. Her walls clamp down on them, as I reach, curling my fingers into that spot that will send her over the edge.

"Asher, shit. Don't stop."

She releases a slew of expletives, each of them feeding my ego. How in the hell did I get so lucky to get here? My fingers rub behind her clit while my tongue presses circles on it from the outside. All the while, my eyes never leave her face. She's so close and trying to hold back. It's so beautiful and has me thinking of the many other ways I can get her to cry out. I relish in each of her moans, and when she finally pulses around my fingers, her body convulsing into itself, I release her clit.

"That's it, baby, come all over me."

I lick her from back to front as she writhes from the sensitivity of her orgasm. I don't want to stop, but I'll be coming in this pool if I stay between her legs.

"Do you have any idea how fucking good you taste?"

She shakes her head. I already had a feeling. Her books tell the stories of sexually adventurous women who are in control of their lives and their sexuality, but her initial responses to our mutual attraction tells another. I reach up with the hand that had made her come.

"Taste."

She's tentative at first, but I urge her on with a nod of my head. She takes my hand in hers and licks my fingertips. My cock twitches and I grab it with my other hand. Her eyes lock on mine again as she pulls both of my fingers all the way into her mouth. This time, it's my head that goes back, and I let out a moan. She runs her tongue along the length of them, and I rub myself through my briefs imagining how it would feel to have her mouth on my cock like that.

"If you keep that up, we're going to need to clean your pool."

She laughs and lets my hand go.

"So come up here."

She reaches over and unfolds the other towel, making a space for me next to her.

CHAPTER 25
KASSANDRA

In all my relationships, never have I had someone worship my pussy the way Asher just did. I still can't believe I'm laying here naked in front of him. I need him to get out of the pool. I need him inside of me. When he doesn't move after I spread the other towel out, I take my legs off his shoulders and scoot back until I'm completely out of the pool. Crooking a finger, I coax him to join me.

"I cannot pull you out of the pool as easily as you lifted me out of it."

His smile turns to a laugh, and he jumps out of the pool as smoothly as he glides through the water. I catch a glimpse of his erection through his briefs and feel heat growing between my legs again. I take in his entire body as he stretches out on the towel, his head and feet extending beyond its length. His nearness and the memory of his mouth on my clit have me asking what Shar would do in this situation. Channeling her, I run my hand down his chest and over his nipple that pebbles at my touch. He makes a grumbly noise in his throat causing my eyes to roll and my thighs to clench. Shit, that's such a turn on.

My hand continues over his stomach, and he tenses.

Whether he's ticklish or anticipating what I might do next, I don't know, but his reactions give me a boost of confidence. When I get to his waistband, I lift my hand and find his knee. His groan tells me he wasn't ticklish. My nails graze up his thigh, and his breathing shifts. I let them slide inside his briefs and caress his lower belly. He is both soft and hard there. Without thinking, I lean over and kiss the softest spot. He sucks in air and nearly chokes, a quick cough punctuating his response. Emboldened, I run my tongue across his pelvis. His cock twitches, and my mouth waters. I want to return the favor.

As soon as I pull down the waistband on his briefs, his cock springs free, rigid, and perfect. He's easily seven or eight inches, and the girth matches the brawniness of the man. I turn my body, so I'm on my knees facing him. My fingers slide up the shaft from base to tip, and he grasps my calf. Heat radiates up my leg and settles in my core, my stomach fluttering at the effect I'm having on him.

I can't remember the last time a man responded to me so well. Charles and I were together for so long that the bulk of my memories were, unfortunately, made with him and, prior to that, other men like him. He never wanted me to touch him, or if I did, it was on his terms. Early in the relationship, he was attentive, but it soon became clear his goal was always to have me ready, so he could meet his needs. He'd get me just close enough to be wet and wanting him but never push me over the brink. Everything about Asher is so different. He gives and asks for nothing more than the privilege. I can at least give him pleasure in return.

In a display of confidence I don't quite feel, I mimic my fingers' movements with my tongue. His sharp intake of breath tells me it was the right move. I swirl my tongue around his tip, tasting the tangy sweetness of his pre-come. I take him into my mouth and slowly work his length in and out until the head of his cock touches my throat.

"Ahh yes, baby, like that. Fuck."

I love how vocal he is and try to pull more moans from him by working my mouth up and down his shaft. His breathing is erratic, and his toes curl tightly. His hand has moved up, squeezing my thigh and then spreading my ass cheeks apart, his hand squeezing the one cheek tighter with each of my strokes. Without preamble, he sits up and grabs both of my thighs, lifting me until he has my pussy situated over his face. The man just throws me around like a rag doll.

"Don't stop, Kass. Ride my face, but don't stop," he says from between my legs before burying his face back in my pussy. It is so hard to pay attention to pleasing him when he's working my clit the way he does. I try to focus on running my tongue around his cock as I stroke him with my hands, but then he puts his fingers in me, and I'm transported.

"Shit!"

The abrupt way he stops working my body pierces through the post-orgasm fog. His scream hadn't been one of ecstasy. I try to lift my leg off him, so I can turn around, and he grabs it.

"Careful," he says. "Go the other way."

I don't know what is happening, but I do as he says. When I'm kneeling on the bare patio, he sits up, and there is blood trickling down the back of his head.

"Oh my god, what happened?"

"This little shit attacked me."

He turns his torso in my direction, and there is a ball of gray fur in his hands.

"Oh no, Ferris. I'm so sorry, Asher."

He rubs the kitten's head with a smile, and I barcly hold in a chuckle.

"He wanted you to rub him instead of me," I said, laughing fully now.

"Really now?" His brows lift and he smirks.

"Yes," I say and jump up before he can grab me.

I grab my dress on the way into the house and slip it over my head. I have no idea where my bikini is. It's probably still in the pool. Thankfully, I have a small first aid kit in the downstairs bathroom. We must clean up that scratch. Grabbing the peroxide and ointment, I head back outside. Asher is standing in the doorway with just his shorts on, and I nearly forget why I came inside in the first place. Then I see Ferris come trotting in between his feet and shake my head.

"Sit here," I say, gesturing to my desk chair.

"In the hot seat? Do I get to read what you were writing?"

"Absolutely not."

He laughs, as he sits in front of me. Ferris gives a tiny mewl near his feet, and he puts the cat up on his lap without a word. My heart skips a beat.

"Okay, this might sting a bit."

I pour peroxide on a cotton ball and run it up the back of his head, cleaning the blood until I find the actual scratch. It isn't deep, but cats' nails can do some damage even with slight scrapes. I look down, and Ferris has made himself comfortable on Asher's lap. Grabbing another cotton ball full of peroxide, I squeeze the excess onto the scratch, and Asher hisses quietly.

"I'm really sorry this happened."

He turns the chair around and grabs my hand. "I regret nothing, except maybe that we forgot about the furball here."

I mouth a silent agreement and turn the chair back around, so I can put ointment on the area. Hopefully, that will be enough to stave off infection. I'd hate to see this beautiful head marred permanently. Once I get all the supplies put back away, I lean against the desk watching him stroke the sleeping kitten.

"You have so much patience."

He doesn't respond at first, and I almost think he's fallen asleep too.

"My mother would've died laughing to hear you say that.

Hell, if you saw me at work when Gabby Brewster comes in, you'd never describe me as patient."

"Gabby Brewster?" I don't recognize that name.

"Remember the one who I let ruin our first date?"

I do remember that night vividly. It was the first time he kissed me. It was a night of many first after my entire first year here in this house. I wouldn't have called it a date though. This last thought reminds me of the favor I need to ask him.

"Hey, speaking of dates..."

He looks up at me expectantly. There is something in his eye that I can't quite read. My nerves kick in, and I nearly chicken out of asking. Fear of showing up alone to my parents' anniversary knowing they likely invited Charles overpowers my fear of Asher's answer.

"I need a date to my parents' anniversary party. I realize it's last minute, and you might be too busy to get away for the weekend, but you were such a good fake boyfriend last week, I hoped..." I trail off again.

That look on his face shifts once more. Was that disappointment? Before I can get a better read on the emotion, he looks back at Ferris.

"When is it?"

Hope springs in my chest. "This weekend."

His head snaps up. "As in four days from now?"

I smile sheepishly. "I didn't want to go. I tried everything to get out of it, but Malissa begged."

His eyes soften slightly, though his face is still stiff, like something isn't quite right.

"Like I said, you don't have to go. It is very last minute, and maybe meeting the parents is too much for a fake dating situation."

That look again. What is it?

"What's wrong, Asher?"

He picks up the kitten and holds him out to me. As soon as I pull him against my chest, Asher gets up and goes outside.

I watch through the window as he collects his clothes. He scoops my bikini bottoms from the pool and places them between the towels he's folded before carrying everything back inside. Once he shuts the patio door, I hear the lock click. He puts the towels with my bikini inside on the counter, and he pulls his shirt over his head.

"I'll go," he says, "but I have a couple of stipulations."

My brows draw together.

"We stay together in a hotel."

I easily agree to that. There is no way I'm going to stay at my parents' house for the weekend, especially not with Asher.

"And, we act like we're a couple the entire time, not just at the party or when we're with your family. Can you agree to that too?"

He caught me off guard with that question. How would that be any different from what we'd been doing, what we just did?

"Decide now, Kassandra."

The way he says my name does things to my insides. Before I can overthink it, I agree.

"Great! When do we leave? And what are we going to do with the third wheel there?" He points at Ferris, who is once again asleep in my arms.

"Um, we could take him with us."

He shakes his head. "No, I will find someone to take care of him."

"Not a kennel. He's too young."

"I love that you think we have one of those here."

My mouth drops open, and he laughs. I laugh too knowing it was my grocery deliveries that started this whole thing between us. I may have moved to the country, but I'm still a city girl at heart. I watch Asher. Our shared laughter seems to have relieved some of the strain that was between us, but there's still this sort of wall he's put up.

CHAPTER 26
KASSANDRA

With so much on my mind, I can't sleep. I think about Asher and how quickly the tone of his visit had changed when I asked about my parent's party. I don't even want to go to the party, damn it. Why couldn't he see how hard this whole situation is for me? It would have been much easier had he just said no. Maybe that would have been enough of an excuse to appease Malissa. But he made up those crazy stipulations.

Then there's the bomb of a suggestion he dropped on me out by the pool. Do a live author signing here in town? Is he crazy? People don't want to know that their favorite author is a hermit, though she doesn't live in a cave. I look around my shadowed bedroom with its huge walk-in closet and ensuite. Nope, definitely not a cave. Still, I can see the headlines now— 'M Knightsong, famous author, escapes to a large country estate and doesn't leave her house for a year'—News like that will travel fast, and they won't care how much writing I did during that time.

I climb out of the bed and pick up Ferris who has begun pouncing around the bed, matching my unsettled mind.

Might as well do some writing if my brain doesn't want to shut up enough for sleep.

"C'mon, little guy. You can run around downstairs."

Early the next morning, Mack brought Shar to her hotel. She had a business meeting and photo shoot. Of course, she didn't tell him that. She simply said that she had some things to do for work. He also claimed to have business to take care of when she mentioned how sexy he looked in his impeccably tailored blue suit. As soon as he dropped her at the hotel entrance, she missed his presence. She didn't have time to dwell on those feelings, though, as her ride would be there shortly to retrieve her.

Without a moment to spare, she was showered, dressed, and in the hired car on her way to the tech giant's headquarters. It was off the island, but Shar didn't care. The company was paying for the car and driver, so she took full advantage of choosing a hotel with a beautiful ocean view. She certainly got more than she bargained for this week with that view.

Mack's beautiful face came to her mind as she thought about the dinner they shared last night. She would never think to claim it was a date, but the way he looked at her certainly made her feel like it was more than just two strangers fucking. She shook her head, trying to clear the thought from her mind. It would do her no good to begin imagining something more from what was meant to be a beach fling. She would be going home tomorrow, and today was filled with meetings and a very lucrative photo shoot. If all went well, she would need to give her agent a bonus.

Shar was ushered into the boardroom on the top floor of the high-rise office building. There were already others seated around the table, though she only knew two of them. Her agent had saved her a seat between himself and the photographer with whom she had worked on numerous occasions. She was happy to see him, as he always made her look good.

"Good morning, gentlemen," she said in greeting.

Before she could get comfortably settled, the company owner's administrative assistant came to the door to let them know Mr. Sloan Mackenzie was on an important phone call and would be here as soon as he finished. Shar hated being made to wait for a meeting like this. The delay was disrespectful to the people in the room. Hopefully, this wasn't a bad omen for how the rest of the day would go.

Her phone vibrated, and since the meeting still hadn't begun, she opened the screen. It was a text from Mack.

> Mack: Hey, I just wanted to make sure you made it to work.

> I did, thank you.

> Mack: I know you're leaving tomorrow. Can I see you tonight?

> That would be nice.

She pressed the send button and immediately heard a phone beep right outside the door that was already opening. Thankfully, everyone's attention was drawn to the sound, so no one registered her inaudible gasp as Mack walked through the door looking down at his phone.

"I'm so sorry I'm late. There was something urgent that needed my direct attention."

He walked to the front of the room still not looking up at anyone. A small smile played at the edge of his lips. When he finally put his phone down on the table and looked around, that smile fell, and his eyes widened as they locked on Shar. Her pulse quickened and bile rose in her throat. She didn't play where she worked, and the realization that she had just spent the last two days fucking the man who was signing her paychecks made her wish she hadn't had breakfast. She watched as determination replaced the shock in his eyes.

Mack began going over plans for the new ad campaign that Shar would star in. Across the table from her was her costar, an attractive enough man she couldn't even give a second glance. According to the plan, the two of them would be placed in various scenarios for short video recordings and photo opportunities as a way of demonstrating the potential of the company's new cell phones. In addition to the already contracted salary, each of them would receive a phone with lifetime upgrades.

Shar was only half listening. Though the nausea had subsided, her heartbeat still blasted in her ears. All she could think was that Mack had hired her for this job and then seduced her for the entire week prior. Had this been his intention all along? Did she not get the job on the merit of her previous work?

"Excuse me," she blurted and made her way down the hall to find a ladies room.

Thankfully, there was no one else in the restroom, but she closed herself in the stall just in case. She needed a moment to pull herself together. Did it matter why she was hired? Not really. The contract was still valid. What did matter was the time they had spent together, especially in the last two days. It was the first time in forever that she had started to feel a connection with someone beyond sex. If this was all a ploy by him, what did that mean for that connection and her ability to read people?

That was the part she was struggling with. She would, of course, do the job she had been paid for, but what would this week have cost her? Shar took a few more steadying breaths, left the stall, and splashed water on her face. She was still Sharlene Maxwell, and she could take on anything.

The ladies room was down the hall and around the corner

from the boardroom. The rest of the floor was practically empty, unlike most tech companies she'd seen before where there were cubicles in every corner. Up here, there were just hallways and lines of doors that led to what she could only presume were offices. She made her way in the direction she had come when a strong hand grabbed her arm and pulled her through one of the doors.

"What?"

She took a deep breath, ready to scream, but the person twirled her around until her back was to their chest and put their hand over her mouth.

"Don't scream, pretty. It's just me."

Her breath was ragged, partially from the surprise and partially from the awareness that she was held tight against him. She forced herself to relax, though, so he would let her mouth go.

"Mack, what's all this about?"

She hadn't planned to ask him. Honestly, she was never going to speak to him again once they left that boardroom. Now that they were alone in a room, however, she couldn't let it be.

"What do you mean," he asked against her ear before trailing his lips down her neck.

"Stop it," she screeched, spinning out of his arms. "Did you plan this when you hired me?"

"What the fuck are you talking about?"

"This week, seducing me, not telling me that you are my fucking boss!"

"You think I knew that?"

"Didn't you? It's your signature on my fucking contract. My headshot was included in the packet my agent sent."

He released her completely. "You're right. I should've known."

Tears stung the backs of her eyes, but she refused to cry. She would not feel sad about any of it. She would not feel guilty about any of it. She did not know who he was, so the guilt was not hers to bear. She turned to leave the room but stopped.

"I will fulfill the terms of my contract, but I just want you to know I don't fuck where I work."

With that, she snatched the door open and walked back to the boardroom to retake her seat. She assured her agent that she was feeling much better, and then she willed the time to move faster, so she could get shitfaced alone in her hotel room.

I feel the same way as Shar and quickly pour myself a glass of wine while Ferris runs around the great room. He has started exploring more, spreading his wings to learn this new environment.

"You're doing better than me, little guy."

Maybe Asher's right. Maybe I need to step outside the safety of my house. This is a small town, so it isn't like there will be thousands of people and weirdos will follow me home. I'm in less danger here than I was in the city, right? Then maybe I can also put a stop to the gossip train and maybe make some friends. Okay, that may be pushing it a little far. At the very least, I can meet some of my readers and thank them personally.

CHAPTER 27
ASHER

I slam the door on my way in the house. Neither the drive home, nor time spent at the bar getting something to eat has settled my anxiety. Frustration? What in the hell is this emotion? Why couldn't I just enjoy the woman without making shit awkward? Just because I want her with every fucking fiber of my being doesn't mean that she has to respond in kind.

But she did respond. She responded beautifully. I flop on the couch, not even bothering to go to my room. That fucking bikini. My mouth waters just thinking about how damn delicious she looked in it. And she has no tan lines. How many times have I just missed catching her skinny dipping? My cock twitches at the thought, and I pull it out with a laugh. That little furry pussy was really cock blocking today.

I touch the scratch on my head that's barely noticeable and remember the way she took care of me. Her touch sets me on fire. But not just her touch. The looks she gives when she's trying to let herself go. I love watching her internal struggle and the determination that comes over her face when she's decided to take a chance. I want her to trust me, no, trust herself enough to step out of that comfort zone.

Of course, she did that today. When she took my cock in her hand, I thought I'd died and gone to heaven. When she replaced her fingers with her tongue, I saw stars. My hand starts working my cock. How I had managed to not come down her throat earlier, I have no idea. If not for Ferris, I'd have buried myself inside of her before the evening was over.

Instead, we spent the second half of our time together discussing an extension of the fake dating BS that started at the Dogwood Festival. We literally just had our faces between each other's legs, and she's still wanting to maintain the facade. I'm not sure how much longer I can keep it up. I'm also not sure I can stay away if she never wants more. Grabbing the pillow from behind my head, I launch it across the room.

Laying my head back against the hard arm of the couch, I picture Kass open in front of me on the side of the pool. Her smell is intoxicating, and her taste. There are no words for how good she tastes. Like Ambrosia. I stroke my cock in time to her moans, and when she explodes, I do too.

"One day, this won't be just my imagination," I say to the empty room before I finally fall asleep.

I roll into work just as Louise is opening the grate for customers. She side-eyes me before greeting the first person through the door. I don't need her judgment today. I go to make myself busy in the back sorting the mail that arrived overnight when my cell phone buzzes in my pocket.

> Kassandra: Hey, I forgot to answer your other question yesterday. I was thinking we could leave early Friday afternoon. It's close to a six-hour drive. Of course, if you have to wait until after work, that's fine too.

I shake my head at her attempts to appease me. I hate that someone has made her feel that insecure that she feels she has to make herself small.

> What time do you want to leave?

Kassandra: …

> Don't ask me what time I can go. Tell me what time you want to go.

Kassandra: …

"C'mon, Kassandra," I coax aloud to the empty room.

Kassandra: Okay, let's go no later than 1, so we can get dinner once we get there.

> I'll be there.

Kassandra: And don't forget about Ferris.

> Got it taken care of.

I do not yet have it taken care of, but I will find someone to watch the fur ball. If necessary, I'll ask Jesse, even though I know he knows less about cats than I do. First, Louise has to approve me leaving early Friday and not being here on Saturday. Maybe I should just take the whole day off.

"What's gotten up your back today? Late and grumpy. You haven't done that in a few weeks."

"Nothing, just tired."

She snorts. "Finally took my advice and went after what you want, huh?"

My eyes snap to her, and her mouth pulls back in a silent laugh.

"You know, you can be just as petty as Gabby sometimes."

"If that were the case, I'd have fired your ass a long time ago just on principle."

I crossed my arms. "Then get your firing pen ready. I need to leave early on Friday, and I won't be here on Saturday."

Her brows raise. I expected her to be incredulous, maybe even angry that I haven't given her much time to get coverage. Instead, she looks pleased.

"Going out of town with your lady friend?"

I think about lying to her. I don't want to be the cause of any additional rumors, though, I doubt Louise would be as obliging if I told her those assumptions were wrong.

"Yes. We're going to her parents' anniversary party."

"Holy shit, she's taking you to meet her parents? Already? Isn't that a little quick? Isn't she a little old to be worried about what they think?"

"You're nosy as shit, and all kinds of wrong, Louise. They're having a party. She needed a date. I'm going as her date. End of story."

"Bah," she says, swiping her hand in my direction, as if trying to wipe away a cobweb.

The bell for the door rings, and Louise heads back toward the front. Before ducking out of sight, she turns back toward me.

"I'm not going to fire you. But I need you to come back with a better story than that."

I smile. Then I add, "Oh wait, I need a favor."

She yells out for the customer to give us a second.

"What?" she asks with her arms crossed this time.

"Any chance you can cat sit while we're gone?"

"I beg your pardon?"

"Can you watch a kitten while we're gone? It's too young to be left home alone, and too young for a kennel."

"You have got to be kidding me."

She turns and leaves the room. I yell a thank you at her

retreating back. I'll grab Ferris Friday morning and bring him here for Louise.

CHAPTER 28
KASSANDRA

"I moved to Mission City almost as soon as I got my first real job out of college," I say, making conversation. "Of course, my hometown is a suburb of the city, so I didn't move too far away. Not like you went away to school. I just didn't want to be under my parents' roof anymore."

I knew I was rambling. Something about being back in the city had my nerves all over the place. Being here with Asher created an intense confusion in my brain. I wanted to show him everything, while I also wanted to hide away. Then there was the moment of doubt about staying at a hotel in the city. Would anyone recognize me after all this time? I don't think I've changed much, though I feel like a different person completely.

"I understand the need to get away. In our town, no one really leaves. In general, if you are born there, you will breathe your last breath in the same zip code. I needed to at least know what life was like outside of those rolling hills and dirt roads."

I lay my hand over the one he had on the gear stick. There might be a decade between us, but we have so much in common. I watch his profile, as his jaw works. Perhaps he's struggling with memories as much as I am. He flips his hand over and laces his fingers with mine.

"Have you ever been here before?"

"Once. I rode out here with Jesse and his pa when we were kids. I can't even remember why we came."

"We were here regularly when I was a kid. Again, we lived close, so it was nothing to pop over for a celebration dinner."

The hotel I booked put us almost exactly an hour from my parents' house, and thirty-five minutes from the hall they have rented for the party. It also has its own restaurant. Rather than stopping somewhere on the way, we agree to have dinner at the hotel. The food is decent enough, and I order a glass of wine to take up to the room.

In accordance with Asher's stipulations, we are staying in a room with a king-size bed. I nearly blush when he looks at me with raised brows as soon as the concierge verifies the type of room we want. I will uphold my part of the bargain. I call him 'babe' and lean into him each time he touches my back when we walk through somewhere. It isn't hard to enjoy the benefits of being with Asher. He knows how to make a woman feel special. When we fall asleep fully dressed in each other's arms, I hope I can let the fantasy go when we're done pretending.

The morning comes entirely too early when Malissa calls. I throw my arm over my eyes, as if the sun is bright, but sunrise has barely started. A groan leaves Asher's sleeping form, so I answer the phone to keep it from waking him fully.

"What?"

"Good morning, sunshine." Malissa's cheerfulness is a ruse. I know her better than that.

"You're not more of an early bird than I am, so what do you want?" I refuse to fully open my eyes.

"Can't I be happy my sister is back in town? You are back in town, right?"

I groan into the phone. "Damn it, Lissa, what do you want?"

She laughs ruefully. It is an uncomfortable laugh, and my stomach clenches.

"I made the mistake of telling mom and dad that you are bringing a plus one. They insisted I invite you both to breakfast."

Another groan bursts from my lips waking Asher.

"Is everything okay?" I gesture for him to give me a second.

"What time, Lissa? And where? Please tell me it is out somewhere."

Rather than answer my questions, Malissa whispers into the phone. "Is Asher there beside you?"

If I wasn't so upset about this unexpected meal, I'd have laughed at her ridiculous question. "Where else would he be? I told you he was coming."

"Yeah, but I didn't expect him to be in the same room as you."

"I'm over 40 years old," I say incredulous at her faux prudishness. "Answer my questions, please.

"Ten at the house."

"Fuck me!"

Asher sits up at that with what my grandmother would have called a shit-eating grin. I have to shush him, so I can get off the phone with Malissa.

"So, what prompted that wonderful statement?" he asks, grin never faltering.

I playfully swat at his chest. I hadn't realized it, but sometime in the night, he must have removed his shirt because

162

my hand touches bare skin. My palm tingles at the sensation. I try to pull my hand away, but he catches it. Pulling me toward him, he kisses the inside of my wrist causing heat to flutter in my stomach.

"What time is it?" We both know my question is a distraction technique, and his eyes hold mine steady.

"Just after seven."

I swallow. Plenty of time. Time for what, Kass, my brain teases. Rather than dwell on that question, my thoughts turn to mush when Asher reclines back on his pillow and pulls me with him until I'm half sprawled across his naked chest. The heat that had started in my stomach travels lower until I'm aching for him.

His hand finds my chin, bidding me to look up at him. His gray eyes are dark, like storm clouds, and I lose myself in their depths. I open my mouth to speak, and his strong arms haul me up until our lips meet. Images of us at the pool flash through my mind, and wetness seeps from my core. All this man needs to do is look at me, and I'm a puddle. He never stops at just a look, though. His touch, his mouth, his scent, his taste, it all overwhelms my logic, and I yearn for it all.

Sliding my loose hand up his chest, I wrap it around his neck and pull him closer, deepening our kiss. A growl rumbles into my mouth, and I'm lifted until my body is flush against his. I straddle his hips and break the kiss enough to sit up and pull my t-shirt off. I can't remember the last time I slept with clothes on, and I'm cursing my moment of propriety. His hands grab my hips, rocking them back and forth against him. His eyes close as he takes deep breaths.

I grab his hands and glide them up my waist toward my bared breasts. He watches me intently, and I pull my bottom lip between my teeth. His hips lift us off the bed, and he rolls until he is on top of me. That was not a move I anticipated, and a sharp 'oh' left my lips as I bit a little too hard. I can feel the small swell on the inside of my lip when I rub my tongue over the spot, but I have no time to focus on it because his mouth is on my breast, teasing the nipple with his teeth. His hand is kneading the other one and pinching the taut tip. My head tips back into the pillows. My moans fill the room, and I hope no one can hear me from outside.

"God, you're so fucking beautiful. The way you respond to me...so damn good."

I blush at his praise. Charles had never given me praise. He simply took what he wanted. I wrote Shar's escapades as wishful thinking for what could be possible. I never thought to be on the receiving end. I want more. I want him. Fuck, I want him. I lean up, pulling on his head until I can reach his mouth with mine. He moans into it, as I twirl my tongue with his.

By the time our lips part, we are both panting. He has shifted his legs between mine. He folds me in half, so he can pull my leggings off over my ass. Is there anything he does that isn't smooth as butter? When he releases my legs to the sides, he stares at my pussy, open for him. The look on his face is one of reverence, and I blush again.

"Asher?"

He looks up at me and winks before sinking his body down until his face is fully buried between my lips. My FUPA covers his nose, and I wonder how he can breathe. That thought doesn't matter because in the next second, his tongue is wreaking havoc on my clit, and I'm writhing beneath him. His hands wrap around my thighs to hold me in place as I grind my pussy up trying to increase our contact. His moans urge me closer. They are the sexiest sounds I've ever heard.

"Oh my god. Don't stop."

I feel the tension building in my core, and I buck against his face in need. He takes one of his fingers and wets it with his mouth while using the thumb of his other hand to rub circles on my clit. When he slides it inside of me, I sigh in relief at the sensation. He slowly works it in an out until my legs tense, trying to pull up. Still, he holds me down with his one arm as he slides another finger inside.

"Can you take three, Kass?"

I can't formulate words. He is staring up at me, his hands taking all ability of coherent thought away. I must've done something that signaled agreement because I feel my pussy stretching to accommodate a third finger. I am so open and so close.

"Mmmm so good. Now come for me."

His tongue once again replaces his thumb, twirling circles around my engorged clit until he locks onto it with his lips and sucks. All the while, his fingers fill me, working in and out until my walls clench, and I gush all over his hand.

"Fuuuuckkk!"

He releases my clit. "That's it, baby. You come so beautifully. So genuine."

Between my orgasm and his praise, I'm floating on air, barely registering Asher's shift up my body until his mouth finds mine. I taste myself on his lips, and desire grips me again. I wrap my legs around his waist, trying to pull him into me. His quiet laughter cuts through the lust-filled haze.

"You won't get much satisfaction that way with my pants still on."

I look between us to see that he does, indeed, still have on sweats. My nose wrinkles, and he laughs again. Reaching down, I untie the waistband. He grabs my hands and puts them above my head. I try to pull free, but he shakes his head.

"I have wanted you for so long that if you touch me the right way, I'm going to ruin the day for both of us."

I push out my bottom lip. He shakes his head again and kisses my nose.

"From the sound of your phone call, we do not have all day to enjoy ourselves."

I sigh and shake my head. "No, sadly. Breakfast starts at ten, so we need to leave by nine."

He leans his forehead down to mine. "Then we definitely do not have enough time for what I have in mind."

"Can I have my hands back now, sir?" I ask in as seductive a tone as I can manage.

He closes his eyes and takes a long, deep breath. "One more word, Kassandra, and we won't be making it to your parents."

"Do you want to go shower first?" I ask him.

"That's probably smart," he says and rolls off me.

The sudden loss of his heat has me reaching for the blanket we had somehow thrown to the foot of the bed. I pull it up to my chin to stave off the cold air I hadn't noticed the entire time his body had been against mine. Just as I begin to sink into the warmth, thinking I might doze off for a few minutes, his voice travels through the suite. He hadn't quite closed the bathroom door, and he is singing in the shower. Curiosity gets the better of me, and I climb out of bed. I've still not been able to enjoy the full view of him completely naked, though he's had me fully undressed twice now.

The suite has a huge bathroom with a walk-in shower and separate tub. The shower doors are steamy, but I can make out his shape clearly thanks to the water droplets he splashes on the doors as he washes himself. Suddenly, I am hot from head to toe, and it is not from the steam. I don't have to think twice about what Shar would do because I act strictly on what Kass wants to do. I slide the glass door open and step inside with him.

Asher doesn't notice me at first, so I slide my hands up his back and kiss the middle of his spine. He groans and leans back into me, which is a bit awkward considering our height difference. I slip my hands around his waist.

"Kass," he says in a low tone that is full of desire, "what are you doing in here?"

"Doing what a good girlfriend should do."

He turns around so fast, I nearly slip, but he is faster, catching my elbows and holding me up. He stares into my eyes. There is a question in there that I don't want to consider right now. Instead, with my hands on his chest, I slide down to my knees. He is already hard, and I take him into my mouth.

Our eyes are locked as I work my mouth up and down until the tip of his cock is as far as I can take it on that breath. Relaxing, I push him in further, and his head lolls back. His moan is guttural, and that is all the encouragement I need. I pull up until just the tip is left in my mouth, and I swirl my tongue around it. At the same time, I work the shaft with my hands. He has leaned back so far that the shower is now spraying around him, soaking my hair from the peripheral spray until it is clinging to my face and neck.

"Fuck, Kass. Your mouth feels so fucking good."

Emboldened by his praise, I pull his cock out and slap the tip against my tongue. Looking up, I catch him watching me again. As I take him all the way back in my mouth, he gathers my hair from my face until he has it pulled up at the back of my head. When his grasp tightens, I'm unable to move. The sensation sets my clit to throbbing, and when he starts working his hips back and forth, fucking my mouth, I nearly come undone. I grab onto his thighs to hold myself up as his movements become more forceful. It is all I can do to keep my throat relaxed, so I don't gag.

It doesn't take long before Asher grunts out, "So close, baby. Can I come? Tell me I can fill your pretty mouth."

I can't answer with him at the back of my throat, so I reach up and grab his ass, pulling him into me. That's all it takes for his cock to start pulsing. His yell fills the bathroom, and I come from all the sensations. He lets my hair go, and he pulls his cock from my mouth. So many emotions course through me on the tail of my orgasm, and I don't trust myself to stand right away. Minutes, maybe moments later, Asher's strong hands pick me up.

"Let's get you showered."

I reach for the shampoo, but he grabs it first.

"Let me."

I close my eyes and wait for them to stop burning.

CHAPTER 29
ASHER

I'd be lying if I said I wasn't a little nervous about meeting Kass' parents. She and I still don't know each other well, and there is some kind of strain between Kass and them. Hopefully, they won't ask me any specific questions. I wish she would have let me drive. At least then I could've had something more to think about.

"Hey. Penny for your thoughts."

I smile at her. She looks gorgeous in her cropped pants that hug her curves just right and white button down. She left her hair down, and the waves frame her face. Every inch of her, down to her light pink toes peeping through her pumps is perfect.

"My thoughts are worth a whole lot more than a penny."

She blushes, and I grab her hand to kiss it.

"Is there anything I should know, or questions I should be prepared for? I have the feeling that your relationship with them is a bit strained, and I don't want to cause more damage."

Her brows furrow in the way they do whenever I ask a question she hadn't considered before. Her features shift, and she turns off into a rest area. She parks in one of the most remote spots, turns off the car, and turns toward me.

"You have a knack, you know."

I swallow and prepare. For what, I don't know.

"You manage to remind me that I am not as detailed in conversation as I am in my books."

I laugh. "I think you do alright. I also think your books are quite, um, detailed too."

"Smartass. I'm trying to say I owe you an apology. I've brought you all the way out here without even so much as a conversation of what to expect. I completely understand if you don't feel comfortable going."

I turn my body toward her and grab her other hand, so I am holding both. "I'm here because you said that you needed me, and you're not exactly the damsel in distress type."

One corner of her mouth pulls up into a half smile. I give a light chuckle, coaxing the full smile from her. Then I kiss both her hands in turn. There is little I wouldn't do to see her smile.

"Do you remember our first date?" I make air quotes around the last word. "When I got upset about Gabby Brewster showing up at the restaurant, your words to me were, 'I'm not worried about gossip, but I don't want to stay if you're uncomfortable.' Well, I don't want to do anything to make you uncomfortable."

Her eyes get misty before she looks down. I tilt her chin back up and place a light kiss on her lips.

"You really are the sweetest guy I've ever met, Asher McNeil."

She sits up straighter, turns back toward the wheel and turns the car on. I expect to once again be left with my thoughts, but she surprises me. She's always surprising me.

"Things are strained between my parents and me. They really bought into the nice guy routine of my ex, Charles. They liked him so much that when I called things off, they tried everything to get us back together. They are the real reason I moved so far away. I had a hard enough time getting his voice out of my head without them constantly telling me that I was crazy for leaving him."

She never takes her eyes off the road, but I can tell she's far away. Having an intimate breakfast with her parents is going to be far more difficult for her than anything I was imagining.

"He was terrible for me, for my mental health and my self-esteem. That day you came by, and I freaked out, nearly leaving you holding all my packages on the porch, I heard his voice again for the first time in nearly two years. I had wanted to invite you in, but all I heard was him saying 'you're not main character material, Kass.'"

"He's wrong, Kass. So wrong."

Her lip quivers, and I want to pull her into my arms. I want her to see what I see. I want to kick this guy Charles' ass.

"When I was reading your book that night, I couldn't put it down. Do you know why?" I waited until she shook her head before continuing. "The whole time I was reading, I pictured you as Aurelia. I hardly knew you then, but I saw the connection. You're both strong but vulnerable, sweet yet snarky, and when you described her moaning in ecstasy, I saw your face." I still haven't told her I've read more of her books.

We stop at a traffic light, and I touch her chin lightly. "Look at me, Kass." When she finally turns her head, I say, "You're so much more than I had even imagined."

"Thank you." A tear runs down her cheek, and I brush it away.

Kass' parents' house is about the same size as hers, though less traditional, but so much is different. Their footprint is smaller, and the third floor covers the entire foundation, making it look more institutional than homey. The stonework is impeccable, and the landscaping screams professionally tended, which tells me that appearances are everything. Nothing on the outside says warm, friendly, or welcoming.

When we pull into the driveway, I am ready to defend her from anyone.

Laura and Frank Ross are nothing like I expected, having met both of their daughters. Frank is unexceptional looking with his salt and pepper temples and dyed black hair. He comes to maybe my shoulders and is unimposing in an outfit more appropriate for a regatta than brunch. Malissa obviously gets her height from him because both Kass and their mother are on the taller side. In her kitten heels, Laura sees over her husband's head. Both Malissa and Kass get their eye shape and hair texture from their mother. Neither her bleach blonde crown nor the newly botoxed forehead take away from the fact she was obviously a stunner in her youth.

Their greeting is more subdued than I imagined considering how bubbly Malissa was when I first met her. They each shake my hand warmly and take turns hugging Kass. Laura appears afraid to let her older daughter go.

"We're so glad you both could join us this morning," Laura says as she leads us through the main floor to their enclosed lanai.

The dining table has already been set for the five of us, and food is piled high on platters. There is bacon and two types of sausage, scrambled eggs and a soufflé, pancakes and French toast. There are also three different types of juice, as well as urns set out for coffee and hot tea. Malissa's giggles drag my attention from the huge buffet. She is pointing at me, and I realize my face must have shown my surprise. Kass grabs my hand and invites me to sit next to her.

"Mom's stress response is to cook, usually she just bakes," Malissa says, finally controlling her laughter.

"Usually, it's cookies," Kass adds with a chuckle.

"Y'all really over here just benefiting from your mom's stress," I whisper, at least I think I'm whispering.

"I didn't get all these curves without help," Kass retorts.

My eyes roam over her body before I quickly turn away. If my thoughts travel the same direction as my eyes, I'll need to readjust myself here at the table.

As we settle into our meal, the conversation relaxes, and Kass relaxes. She banters with her sister, which is hilarious, and answers to her parents' questions expand beyond one word. I sit back and observe while stuffing my face with the most amazing pancakes I've ever tasted. They're like magical, buttery perfection. Fluffy with crispy edges. That's why I nearly choke on my last bite when Laura turns to me and asks how Kass and I met.

Kass puts her hand on my knee and offers an answer. "He's my mailman."

Malissa laughs, and Laura scoffs. She was obviously wanting a deeper story. Frank's face hardens like he isn't buying the flippancy of Kass' response. I take a sip of water and try to expand without causing further rifts.

"So, it's not as simple as she makes it sound. I've been her mailman for a year, but we just met a month or so ago."

I pause as her parents settle back into their seats.

"You never saw her in the entire year she's lived there, wherever there is because she still hasn't told us." Frank still sounds unconvinced.

I grab Kass' hand under the table. "No one had. If her name hadn't been on the packages I delivered, no one in town would have known if a man or a woman had moved into the house. The rumor mill was starting to work itself into a frenzy, though, when it became known that she was having her food delivered. That is simply not something that happens in our small town. There was talk of going to the house, sending the police out to make sure it hadn't been taken over by bad guys.

Lots of crazy, small-town talk. I decided that since I go by there almost daily, I would finally knock on the door, and at least give a warning about what was brewing." I smiled at Kass before turning back to her parents. "Then she answered the door in pajamas and fuzzy slippers, all flustered at having had her writing session interrupted, and she took my breath away."

Mollified by my story, her parents withdrew from the table. We survived brunch and left on a positive note, promising to see them all at the big dinner party in downtown Mission City.

"That was a great story you told in there," Kass said almost as soon as we got in the car.

"It was actually the truth."

I watch her out the corner of my eye, as I set the GPS for our hotel. She opens her mouth as if to say something but changes her mind, closing it again. I'm just grateful she let me drive.

CHAPTER 30
KASSANDRA

A nap is exactly what is needed after a morning spent stressing about seeing my parents and then actually spending time with them. Waking from said nap wrapped in Asher's arms just makes it even better. I watch him sleep, his slow and steady breaths a healing balm for my scarred heart. I may not have responded positively to his insistence that we maintain the dating facade throughout the trip, even when we're not with anyone else, but the benefits have been amazing.

The clock ruins the moment, as it is already after five, and we need to be at the venue by six thirty. I bring my palm up to his cheek, and he nuzzles into it. My heart flutters, but we don't have time for my emotional machinations.

"Hey." My voice is barely above a whisper, and he doesn't move. "We have to start getting ready," I say a little louder. His eyes flutter, and he pulls me closer to his chest. There is nothing I want more than to bury my face in the crook of his neck and inhale his scent until I drift back to sleep. Sadly, we made promises earlier, and the sooner we go, the sooner we can leave. "Asher, we need to get up."

"I'm up," he says, pulling my hips against his.

Yes, a part of him most definitely is up. "That is not what I meant, sir."

He does that chest rumble thing that sends heat to my core. It's not quite a growl, but damn if it isn't sexy as hell.

"Call me sir again."

The statement isn't a threat. The promise in it has me weighing the benefits of being on time to the party and of taking our time.

"Can we revisit that when the party is over?" My voice is breathy, and his eyes open fully to stare at me. The heat in that stare is not helping me tamp down the libido.

"What time is it?"

When I answer, I can tell he, too, is weighing the options against the clock.

"We don't have much of a choice, do we?"

"Sadly, no."

"Fine. I will not be held responsible for our tardiness if you join me in the bathroom again."

"I guess I'll just have to get ready out here then."

Getting up, I pull off my shirt. It's not like he hasn't seen me naked more than once now. I need to change out this bra for a strapless one to go with my dress. Before I can reach behind me, though, Asher is there undoing each hook at an excruciatingly slow pace.

"Did I not make myself clear that it would not take much to provoke our delay? Or do you not understand how much this beautiful skin provokes me?"

With my bra loose, he wraps his arms around me, pulling me back into him and turns us around, so we are facing the mirrored doors of the closet. He lets the bra straps slide down and my bra drops to the floor. His hands cup my breasts from behind, and I lay my head back on his chest, exposing my neck and shoulder to his mouth.

"Watch," he says, his voice husky. "Do you see how fucking sexy you are?" He asks against my ear. "Soft in all the right places, perfectly made for these big hands. Yet, you expect to show off this body and me not want to touch it, to taste it."

He kisses my neck and trails his lips down to my shoulder. At the same time, his hands trace down over my stomach, and he unbuttons my pants. My breathing is ragged, as he slides both my pants and my panties off my hips and over my ass. He leaves them both there at mid-thigh.

"Asher, we..."

"Shhh, just watch. Watch me enjoy every beautiful inch of your body."

He wastes no time, bringing his hands inward from where they left the waistband of my pants until he was squeezing my vulva between his hands, kneading the plump mound. His fingers delve in to find my clit, and a moan leaves my lips. He knows how to work my body.

"Mmmm I love that you're already wet for me."

After placing another kiss below my ear, he removes his hands. I protest, trying to hold them in place.

"So impatient, my love? You told me we didn't have time, and then you started stripping. I'm just trying to help."

He squats down behind me and pulls my clothes the rest of the way off, kissing my hip and ass as he takes out each foot, spreading my legs apart in the process. He stands again, leaning around to take my nipple into his mouth. Simultaneously one hand slides to my pussy while the other slips between my ass cheeks. I let out an audible gasp, and he moans against my breast.

"Don't stop watching."

His one hand begins making small circles on my clit. The other slides downward until it finds my opening. He slips two fingers inside of me.

"Asher, shit, baby."

"Listen to the beautiful sound. If you didn't tell me how ready you are, your body would do it for you." He looks toward the mirror. "You're so fucking gorgeous with your bright eyes, flushed skin, and my hands buried inside you."

With every stroke, he pushes me closer to my release. I feel my legs getting weak, but his hands on either side of me hold me up.

"We're almost out of time."

It wasn't a question, but I respond anyway. "Yes."

"I want you to wait to come until we get back."

"What?"

"I want your panties wet the entire time we're gone. I want you focused on something else besides the party."

His hands continue working on me, and it is getting harder to focus on the conversation.

"You're going to have to stop that if you want me to wait."

He looks back into the mirror, and his eyes are impish. His smile adds to the anticipation of what he is planning.

"I'm not quite done yet, Kassandra."

The sound of my name on his lips is just as erotica as his hands between my legs, at least until he adds his thumb to my pussy with his fingers, slipping it in and out. He rubs my wetness around my asshole before he slides his thumb in the tight opening.

"Oh my god, Ash."

The look on his face is feral, and my clit throbs under his fingers. His eyes never leave mine.

"Fuck, you take my fingers so good. Will you take my cock just as good?"

"Yes, fuck. I'm gonna come."

I feel my pussy tightening around his fingers, and his desire is about to push me right over the edge. I want him to fuck me. I want his cock inside of me, but I also want to do what he asked and wait. Shit, I want to make him happy. Still, I whimper when he pulls his fingers out of my holes and away from my clit.

"Not yet, beautiful. That orgasm will be my prize for

tonight, a gift for holding back now when all I want to do is bury myself inside of you." He captures my lips with a kiss that makes my knees weak. "Now, wash up and get dressed before we're late."

By the time we get to the venue, guests are already arriving. We receive a sideways glance from Malissa, but thankfully, the parents are just happy to see us there. As I take my place in the receiving line, since they have decided to make the party as formal as possible, Asher comes up behind me and whispers in my ear.

"I'm going to sit over there and watch that beautiful body move."

I turn so he can kiss my cheek, and then I watch him walk across the wide hall. I'd have never imagined it when I first saw him in his uniform, but damn if he doesn't wear a suit well. I'll have to ask him how he got a suit so quickly, and so well-tailored. I doubt there are lots of reasons to wear them around town. Either way, I will never get tired of watching him walk away.

My sister nudges me in the side. I forgot what I was supposed to be doing, and the line is stopped waiting for me to greet people I haven't seen in years. The one with his hand out now is an old colleague of my dad's. The woman with him is at least fifteen years younger than his wife, or at least the woman I remember to be his wife. I look back to find Asher staring at me, and I acknowledge the twelve or so years between our ages. I guess I shouldn't judge the man too harshly.

"Don't look now," Malissa whispers in my direction.

I should have listened, but no. I look up to see Charles

enter the hall with some woman on his arm. She is wearing a very severe black gown that seems to make her look older, which is probably his doing. When they reach me, he takes my hand and leans in to kiss my cheek with a whisper.

"It's so good to see you, Kassandra. You look better than I remember, almost good enough to eat."

Asher must have noticed my discomfort because he jumps to his feet. I manage to shake my head toward him when Charles pulls back, and he remains by the chair watching us carefully. Ignoring Charles, I greet the woman with him. She clings to his arm and returns my greeting with a curt nod. I remember him telling me that I should not speak. I feel bad for her. As they walk away from me, I see Charles nod in Asher's direction. Asher doesn't even acknowledge Charles. His eyes never leave me. In that moment, I know I will not be happy with things returning to normal at home once our fake dating agreement has ended.

As soon as the initial line ends, and the doors close, I make my way to Asher. He wraps his arm around my waist, and I lean into him. He tries to grab my hand, but I pull away from him.

"I need to go wash my hands. I've not touched that many people in so long, I probably have cooties." I wink and walk away to the washroom.

He is waiting for me when I return, and there is a question in his eyes as he takes me in.

"I'm okay," I say, and I mean it. Asher's presence makes seeing Charles so much easier than I thought it would be. If I'm honest, his presence makes everything so much better. That thought has me closing my legs together, as the image of our mirror play comes to mind.

Dinner goes smoothly enough. My parents beam at the room full of guests, and they bask in the congratulatory speeches. Malissa sits to my right swiping tears off her face every couple of minutes. I clap along with everyone. They really are a great couple and so good for each other, and I hate that there's been a rift between us. I'm pulled from that thought by my cell phone buzzing. No one ever calls me. I pick it up, and there's a text from Asher.

Asher—The way that dress is hugging your ass makes me want to take you in another room.

He puts one hand on my thigh and the other on my back, right above the curve of my ass. My skin burns through the fabric, and my clit throbs in response to the circles he's making at the base of my spine. I look over at him, and he is staring straight ahead, watching the person giving the speech. I've not heard a single word spoken, and all I can focus on now is his hand moving up my thigh under my dress.

I take my phone and type in the message 'is this why you were so happy I was wearing a cocktail dress?' Rather than click send, I turn the phone toward him, so he can read it. His laughter rumbles next to me before a quiet 'yes' is breathed at my ear. My pussy spasms, and I excuse myself to the bathroom.

Applause emanates from the dining hall when I exit the restroom after getting myself under control again. I smile at how well the evening has gone. Maybe all my worries were unfounded. Then a voice comes from behind me.

"Who's the guy who keeps putting his hands all over you?"

My stomach clenches and my nostrils flare at the possessiveness in Charles' voice. Two years apart, and he still can't take a hint. I turn to face him.

"That's none of your business."

"You never liked public displays of affection."

I laugh, and I'm sure I sound unhinged. "None of your public displays were ever affectionate. They were only done for personal benefit, your benefit." I try to make my voice as acidic as possible, but he just steps closer.

He sneers, before responding with his own special air of

superiority. "If you had been smart, you'd have realized that anything benefiting me would eventually have benefited you. You could have been someone worth knowing."

"I'm not having this conversation with you. You're not worth it."

I turn to walk away, and he grabs my arm so tightly, I'm jerked to a halt.

"Don't walk away from me, Kassandra."

"Don't get that arm broke."

Charles turns toward the voice, but I don't need to; I know who's there. He looks between me and Asher and lets my arm go.

"I believe the lady said she was finished with your conversation. I doubt she even wanted to talk to you at all."

"We have history, and our conversation is none of your business."

"Her happiness. Her safety. Her future is my business." Asher turns to me. "Are you happy talking to this guy? Do you feel safe? Do you want him in your future?"

Bolstered by Asher's presence and pissed at the discomfort in my arm, I answer, directing my words at Charles, "No, no, and hell no."

"Then we have no more business here," Asher says, offering me his arm. "Oh," he says, turning to face Charles again, "and if you ever touch Kassandra again, I will do worse than fulfill my promise of breaking your arm."

Charles storms back to the dining hall before we could turn back that way ourselves. He leaves moments later, dragging his date by the hand. I feel Asher tense, anger radiating from him at their fleeing forms. I put my other hand on his arm and shake my head when he looks down at me.

"I wouldn't have appreciated anyone stepping in when I was in the middle of it with him." The adrenalin from the incident was starting to wear off, and my voice was much lower than it needed to be, drawing his full attention.

"Are you alright?"

"How much of that did you hear? The conversation, I mean?"

His gaze was earnest when he said, "Enough." He pulled me into his arms fully. "You did so well and totally held your own. If he would've never put his hands on you, I wouldn't have stepped in at all."

"Really?"

"Baby, you were brilliant and strong. I still want to break a pitchfork off in his ass, but you were great!"

"Can we get out of here?"

"Absolutely. Let me go grab your stuff and tell Malissa what's happening, so she can let your parents know."

I grab his hand before he can walk off. Pulling him down to me by his lapels, I whisper a quick thanks and place my lips on his. He deepens the kiss just a bit before he lets me go and walks into the dining hall. Within minutes, we are in the car and on our way back to the hotel.

CHAPTER 31
ASHER

We make the thirty-minute drive in relative silence. I hold her hand the entire time trying to tether her to the present. I want to tell her how proud I am of her for how well she handled herself, even more than I conveyed back in the receiving hall. It had been all I could do to not tackle him to the ground the moment he told her that she wasn't someone worth knowing. She's literally the most interesting woman I've ever known, and lots of people in our town would love to meet her. I'm not a knight in shining armor, though, and she's not a damsel in need of saving.

I turn to look at her at a stoplight and find her staring at me. Her faraway look is fraught with uncertainty, and I wish I could take it all away. Would she trust me to do so?

"Quarter for your thoughts?"

When she refocuses on me and lets out a chuckle, I can't help but laugh.

"I don't deserve you," she says, and my face must speak my confusion because she immediately continues with, "I only offered you a penny for yours this morning, and here you are offering me a quarter."

My laughter rings through the car, and I'm sure the people

right next to us must think I'm crazy. When the light changes, I sober enough to continue the few blocks we have left. "After the day you've had, I figure your thoughts are worth so much more."

She covers my hand with her other one. "I was literally thinking how much I appreciate you and everything you've done this weekend. I'm not sure I would have survived it alone."

I shake my head in response and say, "You would have. You're so much stronger than you give yourself credit. But I'm glad I was able to be here with you. Thank you for inviting me." I didn't add the thought my brain conjured. Finishing with 'even if it was just to trick your parents' might just ruin the whole night. Instead, I bring her hand to my lips. It is so hard not to touch and kiss her whenever she's nearby. For all that this weekend has gone so well, it is simply going to make things harder when we get back home and go back to our normal mailman-author lives.

Pulling into the parking lot, I push all those thoughts away and try to focus on the time we have left here. I have one more night with her in my arms pretending this is all real, that there's something more than just sexual attraction. Because damn am I attracted to her. The sway of her hips in that dress has my pants uncomfortably tight.

She beats me inside because I'm taking my time fixating on her ass, and she stops at the concierge desk. When I step up to the counter with her, she grabs my hand and pulls me toward the elevator.

"What's the rush?"

"Can I not be in a hurry to get you alone?"

I shake my head with a laugh, but I let her pull me along. This is a different mood from the one she had when we left the dinner. When she looks up at me while we wait for the elevator, my cock gets hard. The desire in her gaze is palpable. And when she takes my tie from inside my jacket and pulls me into the elevator, I have no more thoughts. That's a lie. I have lots of thoughts.

As soon as the door closes, she stalks toward me. Stalk is the only word to describe my body's response to her movements.

"You got me thinking," she says. "I've spent so long focused on surviving that I haven't even considered what it would feel like to just live." She walks her hands up my chest and reaches them around my neck as best she can without me leaning down to meet her. "And the first step in living," she purrs, as she comes up on her toes and pulls me down to her, "is showing you just how damn much I have wanted you."

Our lips crash together because now it's not just her desire but mine as well. I reach down and wrap my hands around her ass, pulling her up until she wraps her legs around my waist. Her gasp says she's never had anyone do that before, and it drives me crazy wanting to give her all the firsts a woman like her should have had many years ago. When the elevator opens, I carry her down the hall, my lips never leaving her skin.

"You're going to hurt yourself."

"Baby, I've picked up dudes way bigger than you and thrown them across a field. My only plan is to throw you on the bed."

My jacket has long since come unbuttoned from her movements where I have her pinned to me, and my shirt is damp where her sex touches my waist. The wet seeps through the material and I remember my earlier request.

"You're not going back on your promise, are you?"

She freezes in my arms as I take the keycard from my back pocket to open the door. Her strong legs never slip when I let that side go.

"What promise?" she asks when the door slips open.

"That you would not come until I do."

I capture her mouth again with a growl and close the door with my foot. She shakes her head against my cheek. I lay her on the bed, and untangle her legs from my waist, rubbing my hand between her thighs to her wet panties. They are soaked.

"My shirt tells a different story," I say, standing to my full height and removing my jacket.

Her mouth goes wide at the sight of the clearly wet spot on my white shirt. The material is damn near transparent. With her eyes low, she gets up from the bed, and stops my hands where I had begun to undo the buttons. She kisses my hands and turns us around, pushing me to sit on the bed. Dropping to her knees in front of me, she pulls the shirt out of my waistband and begins the slow process of undoing the buttons with her teeth. By the time she gets to where it is soaked with her juices, I'm ready to impale her on my cock.

"That's so fucking hot."

No sooner do I get the words out that there's a knock on the door.

"Who is it?" I snarl and she laughs.

"Now you know how I felt all those times I was interrupted right at the good parts." The wriggle of her nose as she rises to her feet makes me laugh.

"I'll get you for that, my pretty."

"And my little cat too?"

"Definitely."

She comes back from the door with a bucket of ice, a bottle of chilled wine, and two wine glasses.

"Damn, I love the way that dress moves. Your damn body keeps me up at night."

Looking over her shoulder, she gives me a wink and finishes pouring the wine. She hands me a glass and sits in the armchair near the table.

"Tell me more about what you do when you're up at night because of my body." She sips the wine.

I also take a sip from my glass and smirk. Two can play this game, I think while yanking my belt off in one fluid motion. The idea of putting it around her wrists like she described in the most recent book of hers I read has my cock aching to escape the confines of these dress pants. I let it out, my eyes never leaving hers.

"You want to see what I do, Kassandra?"

She nods, and rubs her hand up her neck, biting on her pinky nail as I wrap my hand around my shaft. I slowly slide my hand up and down the shaft, and when I bite my lip at the sensation, she shifts in the chair.

"Do you ever think about me when I'm not around, Kassandra?"

I love the way her eyes shift whenever I say her name. I've called her many pet names the past few days, but nothing gets a reaction like her name on my tongue.

She nods. "Yes." And that one word is little more than a breath.

"Take off the dress. Show me what you do when you think of me."

She purses her lips, as if she considers saying no, but when I stop stroking myself and finish removing my clothes, she puts her glass on the table and stands. Turning around, she opens the small buttons at her neck. They're the only thing holding the dress on and all I could think about all damn day. The material slides off her shoulders and down over her ass. She has to use her hands to get it past her hips, and her squirms have me grabbing my cock again.

"Mmmm so perfect."

She once again sits in the chair and refills her glass for another sip. Her eyes are fixed on my cock, watching as I work it up and down, pre-come glistening on the tip. Her free hand rubs from her neck to her chest and into her bra cups, first one and then the other. I should've had her take that damn thing off.

"Show me," I say, my voice stern.

Finishing the last of her wine, she sets the glass aside and unhooks her bra. Once it's on the floor, she throws one leg over the chair's arm, opening her legs to me, the sheen of wetness on her panties.

"Take them off."

She turns her head a bit to the side, and I want her to be defiant. My cock strains with how badly I want her to say no. I'm not sure she's ready for that, though, I have no doubt she could be. She's been surprisingly aroused at every other thing I've done. When she finally complies, I'm torn. Her naked pussy open is a beautiful sight, but I still have the desire to see how her defiant side handles a spanking.

Her movements bring my attention back to the present, and I put that dream away for another day. The way her nipples pucker after she rubs against them leaves me drooling, and when she slides one hand down to her pussy, my breath catches. Her mouth opens slightly as she rubs circles on her clit. Within minutes she dips her fingers inside, and I hear that glorious wetness. A moan leaves her mouth at the same time I finish off my wine and land on my knees in front of her chair.

I hold her hand in place, adding one of my fingers to hers. At the same time, my tongue wraps around her clit, sucking it between my lips. I nearly forget myself and lean up to slide into her. I reach over for my bag, which is on the floor, and pull out a condom. I remove my hands from her and sit back on my knees.

"Come here." I reach for her hand and pull her off the chair to stand in front of me. Holding my covered cock up straight, I say, "I want you to ride me."

She looks me up and down, but it doesn't take her long before she's grabbing onto my shoulders and lowering herself into a squat. She's incredibly wet, and yet it still takes a couple of bounces before she's seated completely on my cock. Her breath hitches, and I bite my lip at how incredible she feels. I don't want it to be over before it begins. Small movements become larger and needier.

"That's it, baby. Take what you need."

My libido has always responded to her moans, but the way it reacts now, knowing it's my cock she's riding is something else entirely. I reach around and grab her ass, moving her up and down on my lap, guiding her to almost pull it out completely before slamming her back down on me. Every thrust pulls the sweetest sounds from her. Her slick walls start to tighten, and there's no way I will survive her orgasm in this position. Not when I already feel every beat of her heart and every breath she takes in.

Wrapping my arms around her waist, I stand up from the floor and move to lay her on the bed. She doesn't protest as much as I expect, probably because I never pull out of her. That part is not as easy as I had hoped, but I'm able to slide back in fully as soon as I pull her ass to the edge of the bed. She puts her legs up on my shoulders, and I thrust in and out, controlling the friction. I've been waiting too long to be inside her to be happy with a quick finish.

"Asher."

I love that she always starts with my name as she chases her release. With my hands around her lower back, I lift her up and climb up on the bed, so I can hit a different spot inside of her. Her body is folded in half, and my cock rubs the ridge that makes her scream. Neither of us is going to last much longer, as her walls clench around me, and my balls tighten. Her moans come with every thrust, and my breathing is ragged.

"Fuck, Asher, don't stop."

"No way, baby. It's time for you to come for me. Take me with you."

There's no way I could stop now. I need this as much as she does. She reaches, trying to pull my ass tighter against her, and I know she's so close. Reaching between us, I find her clit with my thumb. Within seconds, she is pulsating around my cock, drawing my orgasm with hers.

"FUUUCK, Kass." My cry drowns hers out, and I collapse

on her chest, letting her legs fall off to my sides. "My god, that was glorious."

She giggles, and I laugh with her. I somehow manage to get myself off the bed and shuffle to the bathroom on wobbly legs. When I come out, she's naked in the middle of the bed ordering a pizza.

"Hungry?"

"Famished."

I climb onto the bed and lay my head in her lap.

I have never felt so alone walking into this empty house. Kass' scent lingers on my skin and in my system. I don't know what I expected when I dropped her off at the house tonight, but I guess I wanted more than for her to simply ask when I was bringing Ferris home. The weekend had been so good, and we were so good together. Does she see that? Can she feel that?

Fuck the sex. While it is amazing, there's something more there, a connection. That will be the hardest part to let go.

Flipping on the TV, I flop on the couch and try watching a home improvement show. Watching the couple work in tandem to create something beautiful doesn't make me feel better. I pull out my sketch pad and start working through a new kitchen design for the house. It's about time I start thinking about getting my life together.

I wake for work with a groan. One of these days I'll remember that sleeping on the couch is no good for my damn back.

Rolling to my feet, I search for my phone to check the time. It was under the edge of the couch. How the hell it got there, I have no idea. Fifteen notifications? What did I sleep through?

> Kassandra: Hey. Is everything okay? You left so fast.

> Kassandra: Did you make it home alright?

> Kassandra: Asher?

> Kassandra: um, I hope you're just asleep.

> Kassandra: I hate that this weekend had to end.

A knot forms in my throat. What does she mean by that last text? Do I want to know? Fuck. I can't think about that this morning. I need to get ready for work. I scroll past the rest of her texts and find one from Jesse and one from Louise.

> Jesse: Hey, you don't happen to have Malissa's number, do you? Any chance you can get it for me. I can't stop thinking about her, man.

I can't even think about that right now. There is no way I'm going to play matchmaker between my best friend and my girlfriend's sister. Shit, no, she's not my girlfriend. She's not my anything. She's my damn customer. She's the woman I share a fucking cat with. She's the woman I can't get enough of. She's the woman, the woman I want to be with. Dammit! What did Louise want? Hopefully nothing to do with Kassandra.

Louise: Just checking to make sure you all made it back in time for you to come to work in the morning. What do you want me to do with this kitten? Bring him to work?

"Fuck me sideways," I say aloud to the empty room. I drop my phone on the couch and head upstairs to shower.

CHAPTER 32

KASSANDRA

I've not even sat at my desk for days. Shar's story is finished. My publishing contract is completed. I don't even know where I want to go next. There's no point in staring at a blank screen and wishing for the mail to come. Who knew that a kitten could take up so much space in a house that it would be empty without him there? I miss the little furball, and I've just about given up hope that Asher will bring him back.

The sounds of a vehicle coming up the drive penetrate the house. I rush to the door and watch as a white truck comes into view. My heart races. But it's not Asher behind the wheel. It's someone I've never seen before. It takes everything in me to not slam the door shut, but the driver waves in that polite small-town way. I plaster a smile on my face and meet him before he even gets out of his truck.

"Afternoon, ma'am."

"Good afternoon to you. I almost thought I wasn't going to get any mail this week."

"I'm sorry, ma'am. I'm just filling in for the regular carrier."

"Oh, is something wrong with Mr. McNeil?"

"Asher? Oh no, he just took the week off unexpectedly."

"Oh good. Glad to hear nothing's amiss. I appreciate you making the trip out here."

He hands me one package and says his goodbyes. I hold in a sob until the truck is out of sight. He's okay, but he's ignoring me. And he's keeping Ferris. I let the tears run, as I walk slowly back inside, mindlessly opening the package in my hand. It's my proof of Shar's final story. I'm losing everything all over again. Shar, Ferris, Asher. Fuck my life.

I open my laptop to see if there's word from Malissa about the book. She has beta read all Shar's books, so I couldn't keep this last one from her, even though it is so different. Right there on the screen is her response, sent days ago. I open it and immediate bust out laughing through the tears that haven't fully stopped. Rather than read through her diatribe, I pick up the phone and call her.

"What's wrong?" Malissa asks after picking up on the first ring.

"Why does something have to be wrong," I retort trying to hide a sniffle.

"You never just call, like ever. What's wrong?"

"I saw your email and figured you'd like the opportunity to tell me off yourself." I chuckle, and it sounds fake even to my ears.

"Kassie, what's wrong?"

"Please just talk to me about the book. Please."

After a slight pause, she does tell me her thoughts about the book. She was shocked at how careless Shar was with her own safety. Shar was usually so meticulous in researching people and locations, not trusting anyone, especially men, to do right by her. The second half of the book, though, went against everything Shar normally stood for. I'm pacing in front of the island by the time she finishes her recap of everything that seemed out of character.

"When did you start writing the part where she met Mack?"

Malissa's question catches me off guard. Why should that matter? "Over a month ago. Why?"

"Wasn't that right when you met Asher?"

Was it? "Maybe."

"Oh Kassie, you got it bad."

"What are you talking about?"

"Shar has been tied to your insecurities for so long, you can't separate her from yourself."

"What do you mean? Shar's never been insecure."

"No. She's been what you wanted to be. As you became more secure, though, she found someone to attach herself to. You wrote yourself and your actual hopes and uncertainties. You wrote your changing feelings for Asher into the story."

I sat on the edge of one of the chairs. Could she be right? Was Shar's pain my pain? Was her story my story? If so, what did that mean? More so, what does it mean now that Asher's no longer in my story?

"Kassie, are you there?"

"I'm here," I say around the knot in my throat.

"Does Asher know how you feel?"

"It doesn't matter."

"What the fuck do you mean it doesn't matter?"

"He dropped me off the day we left, and I've not seen or heard from him since."

"And you've not gone to look for him? Are you crazy?"

"He's been ignoring my texts. He obviously doesn't want to talk to me."

"Kassandra Gingham. You may be my older sister, but you are acting like a child right now. That man is head over heels for you. If he isn't answering it is because he's afraid you don't care."

"What?"

"I said..."

"No, I heard what you said, and I gotta go."

I end the call and jump back on the laptop. I vaguely register an email from the town library when I went looking for Malissa's feedback.

"Yes!" I yell at the screen.

For the first time in days, I feel hopeful.

I plug the address into the GPS and take a deep breath. I can do this. I've only driven through downtown once, and I barely registered anything along Main Street. I nearly choked to find that the post office and the library were adjacent to each other. This could either make the next couple days much easier or really awkward. Hopeful, Kass, hopeful. I've been playing this mantra on repeat since yesterday.

I pull into one of the slanted parking spots right outside the front door. My palms are sweaty, and my heartbeat is racing. I can do this, I remind myself. I grab my stuff and walk in the front door. There are two women standing at the counter. One works there, and I recognize her. The other, a much older woman, turns when the bell sounds.

"Kassandra, right," says the woman behind the counter. "I never expected to see you in here."

"Truthfully, I never expected to be in here either." I chuckle, but neither woman so much as cracks a smile. "I need to send a package."

"I know you know that you could have just given that to the carrier who delivers to your house."

"Yes, I know, but..." I trail off, remembering the other woman is literally standing at the counter. "I'm sorry, I don't want to jump in front of you," I say to her apologetically.

"You're not," Louise responds. "This is Gabby Brewster. She pops in to keep me company most days."

"Oh."

I recognize the name and barely hold back a sneer. She's the woman who caused Asher all that pain years ago. She's the one who nearly ruined our first date. She's the one who had the nerve to talk about my damn grocery deliveries. Breathe, Kass. You're not here for her.

"What do you need, Kassandra?" Louise asks. Her tone is cold. She wasn't the warmest of people when I met her at the steakhouse, but this was on a whole different level.

"Have I done something to you?"

"To me, no. But you're standing in the middle of my post office looking like you want to run or scream, not sure which one." Her lips are pursed.

I take a deep breath. "I need to send this package, but I don't have the full address. I was hoping you could help me with that."

I pass her the perfectly wrapped book with Asher McNeil written on the front of it. She scowls before looking at me. "Is this a joke?"

"No, it's not a joke."

"He hasn't been with you all this time?"

"No, I have not seen him since we got back to town."

"So, what the fuck did you do to him?" Gabby asks, and the woman's gravelly voice grates on me.

"I'm sorry. How is my business any of yours? As for that? How is Asher's?"

"Little girl, I've known that boy since he was in his mother's womb."

Little girl? My parents taught me manners and to respect my elders, but today is not the day. "And? That gives you the right to access all parts of his life? That gives you the right to ruin his relationships, so he's left heartbroken and questioning his worth? That's what having known his mother affords you, you bitter old biddy?"

Louise's jaw drops, and Gabby's slams shut. The woman looks down at the counter and slowly leans her weight onto the stool just behind her. She looks deflated, and I don't know what just happened.

"That girl didn't deserve him," Gabby says quietly.

"What?" I ask, unsure I heard her correctly.

"She didn't deserve him. She was already cheating on him and pregnant."

My mouth drops open. What in the world? "He says you told her that he was cheating and showed her a picture of him at school."

Gabby lifts her head up and squares her shoulders. "I did. When I found out that Carolyn was running around with that boy from a couple towns over. I didn't want her leading Asher on, holding onto him, bringing him back here where no one ever seems to escape." She looks at Louise who is still slack jawed, as if she knows none of this. "I'd have rather he be mad at me for the rest of his damn life than get stuck here with that good for nothing Carolyn Marsh. But then his momma got sick, and he came back anyway."

The knot in my chest returns, and my words are much softer now. "You can't take away someone's agency to make their own decisions just because you see potential hurt in their future." I shake my head and turn my attention back to Louise. "So no, I haven't seen or heard from Asher, and I don't know where he lives. I just know that he had wanted to read this book the last time he was at the house, and I want him to have it. You don't have to give me his address; I wouldn't ask that of you. I'll pay the postage now, and you address it yourself."

Louise looks down at the parcel and nods. "No postage necessary. I'll make sure he gets it."

I put my wallet back in my purse. "Thank you. Both of

you." I turn to leave but then immediately turn back. "Oh, I heard that you are both book lovers. I have it on good authority that there will be a surprise event at the library on Saturday. I'm sure my sister told you I'm kind of an author myself, so I know some people who know some people." And with that, I head home, my thoughts on young Asher with his broken heart so far from home.

CHAPTER 33
ASHER

A pounding on the front door breaks my concentration. I look at the plans laid out across the kitchen table. I'm going to have to start my calculations all over. The knock comes again. "I'm not expecting anyone, are you?" I ask Ferris who has lifted his head from where he's been sleeping in my lap. He lets out a small cry in response. "I didn't think so." The only person I've seen all week has been Jesse. When I never answered his text, he stopped by.

"Asher McNeil, I know you're in there."

Louise's voice penetrates the door and the two rooms between said door and the kitchen. I told her I'd be back to work on Monday. I roll my eyes and stand up. Ferris protests, so I put him on the floor.

I open the door just as Louise raises her hand to knock again.

"What in the hell took you so long?"

"I was doing something." I look down to see Ferris trying to climb my pants, so I grab him up into my arms.

"Hey, little guy," Louise coos. "Are you going to invite me in?" she asks, her attention back on me.

I back up and gesture for her to come in. Louise has never

come to my house before, so I'm just a little curious as to what she's doing here.

"Have a seat. What brings you here? I'm coming back to work Monday."

She sits on the couch but doesn't acknowledge my question. "You know how sometimes you think things are one way, and then you find out they're nothing like you imagined?"

My eyes shift to her face. Louise has never been one to speak in riddles.

"You're acting really strange, Louise. Did something happen?"

"It was an interesting morning down at the old P.O. today. We had someone unexpected walk in and tell Gabby off."

"What? And I missed that?" I chuckle. Louise doesn't laugh. She always laughs at my irrational disdain for Gabby. Ok, maybe it's not fully irrational, but I know it's a little overmuch after all these years. "What did they lay into her about?"

She brings her eyes to mine. "You."

I had just taken a swig of my soda and started choking. "Me? What the hell?"

"Can I get one of those?" Louise asks, pointing at the drink in my hand.

"Yeah, sorry. I should've asked if you wanted anything. You just caught me by surprise." I walked into the kitchen.

"Well, you got some mail today." She is standing in the doorway when I close the fridge.

"And you couldn't just let Curtis deliver it or leave it for Monday?"

She places the parcel on the table, on top of my blueprints. Not for the first time today, I think how much easier this would all be if I would just buy the damn software and draw it up that way. Easy wasn't the purpose though. Focusing my mind on something else besides...My

202

eyes catch the return name on the parcel, and I look up at Louise.

"Kass was at the post office today?"

Louise nodded. "What's all this?" She gestured at the blueprints.

"Just working out some renovation thoughts." Her head leans to the side, and I shrug with a sheepish smile. "Someone told me recently that I needed to take advantage of sparks when they happen."

"Must've been a beautiful and intelligent person who gave you that advice," she says with a smirk.

"Yes, someone very humble," I retort, and we both laugh breaking through the remaining tension. I grab my pencil and erase a mistake I notice while trying to ignore the book-shaped parcel sitting in the middle of the table. "How was she?"

"She who?"

My eyes shoot up. "You know who I mean."

Louise smiles the first genuine smile since she walked in the door. She takes a seat in the only empty chair available and crosses her legs and arms, casually sipping her soda. I take a couple of deep breaths, but my patience is fading.

"She looked like a deer trapped in the headlights when she first got there."

I pick the papers up from the chair closest to me and plop down. "It's been a while since she'd gone places by herself."

"Explains why she looked ready to run. It took her longer than expected to tell me why she was even there." She again gestured at the parcel.

If Louise is expecting me to open it in front of her, she is sorely mistaken. I am not yet ready to give Kassandra Gingham all my attention again, and I surely am not going to do so in front of anyone else, least of which Louise. Also, if it is a book, I don't want to potentially give away her identity like I almost did with the first book.

Louise continues, undeterred. "Then Gabby opened her

fat mouth, and Kassandra fed the woman her own shoe. My damn jaw was on the floor. Your woman was amazing."

I had been smiling until that last statement. "She's not my woman, Louise. We had a nice weekend, and we fooled her parents like she had asked me to help do."

"Yeah, if you believe that's all there is between you two, you're dumber than we all thought you were for moving back here and staying. No one who doesn't care about you tells Brewster off for causing you heartbreak over a damn decade before they knew you."

"Hold on. Wait. What happened now?"

"When Kassandra said she hadn't seen you, Gabby asked her, in her own damn disrespectfully way what Kassandra had done to you."

"Nosy ass bitch." I slam my soda on the table and quickly grab a towel before it ruins my drawings.

Louise laughs. "That's pretty much what Kassandra said amongst some other choice things. Anyway, I gotta get going. I just wanted you to get your package and check on you. Oh, and tell you I legitimately like that woman of yours."

She stands and walks toward the door. It takes me a second to soak in all she's said before I can follow her out. On the porch, she turns back.

"Oh yeah, she also invited. No, invited isn't quite the right word. She told Gabby and I about a special event at the library happening day after tomorrow. No details, just that she thought we might be interested." She shrugs and walks off the porch to her car.

I walk back in the house and pick up Ferris on my way through the living room. The beautifully wrapped parcel sits on the table like an elephant in the room. Kassandra's name and address are written in one corner with my name in the middle in beautiful script. I grab one end of the twine she's tied around it and pull. It unties and I wrap the length around my hand multiple times. I idly pet Ferris' back as I touch the letters of her name. I chuckle thinking about her telling Gabby off.

"I'm sure your mom was glorious, just like that day she stood up to that asshat of an ex."

I sigh and unwrap the book. Her note slips out when I open the cover.

Asher,

This is the book I was writing the day you knocked on my door. I finished it before we went to my parents, and this is my proof copy. You had wanted to read it when you were here, and I told you no. I don't know what I was afraid of, but I trust you with her.

Kassandra

"Dammit, Kassandra." I toss the book to the side of the table and try to focus back on my blueprints.

⁂

The house is still dark when I wake up. Ferris is curled up on my chest, his deep kitten breaths making him look like a breathing dandelion. Like I could make a wish and blow. My wish is across town and probably asleep. Holding the kitten tight to my chest, I get up from the bed and make my way downstairs. I place him in the little bed I put near his food and litter like I had seen at Kass' house. Guilt eats at me for keeping the cat from her.

I turn on the kitchen light to grab something to drink and see her book still lying where I threw it last night. I pick it up on my way out of the room and flop on the couch. I'm not getting any more sleep anyway. Turning to the dedication page, my heart stops.

Sometimes, you lose yourself and it takes an amazing soul to see what you can't. This book is dedicated to the beautiful soul who saw strength in me that I did not feel and then stood by my side until I could see it too. You completely changed the trajectory of my story by allowing me to write what might be instead of what isn't.

Thank goodness I live alone because tears escape my eyes. Pulling my phone from my pocket, I consider calling her. It's barely 4 a.m., so I put the phone back in my pocket and turn to page one of the story.

Ferris is mewling and trying to climb the side of the couch before I come up for air. The sun is high overhead, and my stomach growls. Noon. Holy shit. Half the day is gone, and damn, this book is so good. The main character, Shar, has just met this surfer guy and invited him to her room. Having read the other books with Shar, I know she'll be kicking him out before the next chapter. I laugh and get some food.

It's nearly 6 p.m. by the time I give up on my drawings. The calculations aren't working out, and my eyes are crossing. Watching these home improvement shows reminds me that I really need some kind of tablet. Doing this by hand, while a helpful distraction isn't as efficient as plotting in an app would be. Something sharp pokes my side when I stretch out across the couch. Oh yeah, Kass's book. I hold it to my chest and watch the final reveal. That lanai gives me some ideas to explore tomorrow, and the master bath, wow. I'd have to knock out a couple walls upstairs, but it would be worth it.

As the next show starts, I thumb through the pages, looking for where I left off. Damn, Shar lets him manhandle her like that and gets turned on by it? That's new. Ha! I love how she submits with attitude. Where in the hell does that guy disappear to? If she had been that good for me, I'd have been right back for more, one night stand be damned.

Ferris complains next to the couch, and I pick him up onto my stomach. He spins in circles and paws at my shirt for a few seconds before curling into a ball. I absent-mindedly pet his back while I try to figure out what's going on with Shar and this no-name dude from the bar. I don't trust him. The closer they get to the end of the night, my anger rises. None of this would be happening if surfer dude would've just been what he knew she needed. It's not like his plan all along hadn't been to get her again.

What the fuck? Her boss? Has he been playing her all along? No wonder things didn't quite feel right. Ugh, Mack, what's your game man? I sit up on the couch. Shar needs someone she can depend on. It's supposed to be you, Mack. What's your next move?

※◆※◆※

Shar sat with her co-star. They were already thirty minutes behind schedule for this video and photo shoot while waiting for some last-minute meeting to end. The contract was nearly completed, and she was ready to go. It had been a long week of shoots, an excruciatingly long week back at the beach again without Mack popping by the hotel to surf or coming by the shoots to check in. According to the gossip mill, he was usually more hands on with things like this. She scoffed. He was probably avoiding her after their last conversation. Good, she thought, it'd be easier to put this whole situation behind her completely if she never sees him again. She'd also be sure to tell her agent that she couldn't work for this company again once it was all over.

Finally, the marketing director, videographer, and photographer walked onto the set. The marketing director, Kevin, was an awkward middle-aged man when things were going well. He was downright disheveled when they were not. As the trio approached the center of everyone waiting, he shifted between his two feet, and alternated shoving his hands in his pocket and rubbing his palms on his hips. The other two looked resigned and ready to work, gesturing commands to their assistants without a word.

"There have been some last-minute changes for today's shoot," Kevin shouted, so everyone could hear him. "This will be the last shoot of the contract. Everyone will still be paid their full amounts, even if they're not needed today. Ms. Maxwell's team will remain. No one else is needed." As rumbles of discontent and concern spread from the other teams, Kevin spoke again. "Remember, everyone will get paid for the day regardless of your participation in this last shoot."

Shar walked over to the photographer and asked what was happening. He shrugged and continued to unpack his lenses. The stylist came to take her back to hair and makeup for touchups. She'd not done anything for the last hour, but if they wanted to fluff her hair and powder her nose again, so be it.

"I hear Mr. Mackenzie is inside getting prepped for today's shoot." One of the assistants said to another.

Shar tried to lean closer to the voices from her chair, but it was hard with the stylist playing in her hair. Their voices modulated up and down, and she could hardly hear them. When she couldn't hold back her questions any longer, she stepped out of her chair in their direction.

"Did you say that Sloan Mackenzie is stepping into today's shoot, as in he will be on camera?"

"Yeah, they say he does this from time to time. That's why he shows up in so many of the ads." One of them answered.

The other chimed in, "Makes sense though. He's just as dreamy as that model they've had here."

Shar walked away from them. Mack was going to be in this shoot, on camera, with her. She wasn't prepared for the slew of emotions crashing through her chest. Excitement at seeing him again. Fear at seeing him again. Confusion. Why would he choose to come today of all days? Why not just wait for the next ad campaign? He'd probably be happier not seeing her again anyway.

"Ms. Maxwell, you're needed on set."

Shar took a deep steadying breath. "I am Sharlene Maxwell, and I can do this." Plastering a serene smile on her face, she walked over to the Raven that was parked in the middle of the set. The car was sleek, black, and screamed luxury. They wouldn't let anyone near it earlier, but she heard it had the softest leather seats on the market. She was afraid to look up the price.

"Shar, you and Sloan," the photographer started before he was interrupted.

"Call me Mack." Shar's eyes rolled.

"You and Mack," he began again. "You will stand here outside of the car with Mack's back toward the front of the car. Mack, you'll be looking down at her. Your hand will be in your pants pocket, and your jacket will be pulled back to display the phone in its holder on his hip. Shar, you will be facing Mack with your arms up around his neck. Your front hand will hold the cell phone against his back. You will be looking up at him."

Shar hated the way they made her feel like a rag doll during these shoots, just as much as she loved her job. Being placed up against Mack, though, made to touch his body and wrap her hands around his neck...it was all so unnerving. Her body tingled wherever it touched his. It was hard being mad at him and hurt, and yet completely...

"That's it," the photographer yelled. "You haven't seen each other in a while, and he arrives to pick you up for your date."

She looked up into Mack's eyes. She expected them to be cold, empty, much like her costar had been on each shoot. Going through the motions but aloof. Mack's, on the other hand, were warm. There was such longing in them that her mouth opened in a silent gasp.

"Yes, Shar, that's the expression. Perfect."

"Perfect," Mack repeated, and she stepped out of his arms, immediately regretting the move when goosebumps formed on her arms. How was it he stole her heat every damn time?

The videographer stepped forward as the lead for this scene. This time, Mack and Shar are both inside the car, supposedly on the way to their date. Whoever said the leather was soft did not do it justice. She could have slept on this cloud. In this scene, Mack had to press talk on the car's control while his phone sat in the raised cup holder. Shar was on her phone scrolling. They would superimpose a social media app on it later. Then Mack would hang up the call and reach over to run his hand up Shar's thigh.

She was glad to have her phone in her hand as a prop. It allowed her to pretend to respond to something she saw online because her body went haywire as soon as his skin touched hers. Her first thought was how much the cleaning bill would cost when she came all over the seat. Her second thought was how little she cared. When Mack turned to her and said, "Look at me," she knew it was all over. Her pussy clenched, and her clit ached for him.

"Cut. Great job you two. You have great chemistry on camera."

Mack looked at her and winked. She sat as stoically as possible. Remaining professional was getting harder and harder with each change.

"For this last scene, there will be much more movement. It is a very intimate scene at the end of the night. You're driving her home, Mack, and you keep looking at her thighs. You've missed her like crazy, and dinner wasn't enough. You pull over into an empty parking lot and pull her onto your lap."

Shar gasped. Unlike with TV shows and movies, she never

got a full rundown of each scene ahead of time. Plans changed all the time, so she usually found out on set, unless nudity was involved. That type of scene was always negotiated as part of the contract and never sprung on her at the last minute.

"Is everything alright, Ms. Maxwell?" the videographer asked.

"Yes." Her voice cracked, and she asked for some water. After taking a drink, she tried again. "Yes, everything is fine. I was just trying to figure out the logistics of getting over there across this console."

"Don't worry," Mack interjected before anyone else could say anything, "I'll make sure you don't get hurt."

There go those conflicted emotions again. He had hurt her already. Yet, her insides warmed thinking about him not only holding her up as she transitioned over there but then her straddling his lap. My god, she was going to have a full-blown orgasm and break down in tears at the same time in the middle of a photo shoot.

"Everyone ready?" The videographer asked them before stepping back and lifting his camera. The photographer would get still photos from her side of the car. Both she and Mack nodded.

Shar again had her phone in her hand and was scrolling, trying to give a good view of the phone for the cameras. She could feel Mack's eyes on her, but she didn't want to look his way.

"I've missed you," he said, and her breath caught.

She knew it was part of the scene but still, his words snatched her heart up. When he reached over and ran his hand up her thigh, under her dress, her heartbeat rose until she was near panting. He took the phone from her hand and threw it in the backseat. Kissing the inside of her wrist, he used his freehand to turn her chin in his direction. "Come here." And she did. Somehow, he lifted her from her side of the car to his lap faster than she could think of where to put her legs.

With her legs on either side of him, her sex pressed against his erection, and fuck was he erect. "Shar." Her name was a plea on his lips, and his eyes bore into hers. "I'm fucking sorry. I didn't know. You don't have to believe me. Hell, I wouldn't believe me because I should have known. Maybe I just didn't want to do the math."

"Stop," she says on a whisper, tears forming in her eyes. "If I start crying, my makeup will run, and all this work will be ruined. The photos, the videos, everything. I don't want everyone to see me cry."

"Hey, there's nobody here, pretty. Just me and you, at least it better be just me and you."

She froze for a second and then looked around. The set was empty, and most of the lights were off. "When? How? Why?" She looked to him for explanation. It was so hard to remain still and focus on the conversation while straddling him, but she needed to know. To his credit, once she was over there, he'd kept his hands off her.

He ran his hand through his hair. "Every day, I would get the plans for the photo or video shoot. I knew you didn't really want to see me, and I intended to follow your professional wishes." She watched him carefully, trying to find any clue that he might be lying. "Last night, I got today's plan, and this scene, as described, was in there. I couldn't. Fuck, Shar, I couldn't fucking sleep imagining you straddling that rando's lap with his hands on your hips. Not for my damn ad campaign. Not when I'd have to look at it and show it in board meetings. Not when I couldn't touch you."

"Mack." Her voice was much firmer this time, and he stopped talking, a question in his gaze. "I need you to touch me."

That was all it took. His hands were all over her. In her hair, pulling her mouth to his. Under her dress, grabbing her ass and rocking her hips back and forth along the length of his cock. Sliding the straps of her dress off her shoulders, so he could suck on her nipples.

"Mack, please."

"Please what, pretty? Anything you want."

"Inside of me now."

He reached between them, and she leaned back, accidentally blowing the horn. They both jumped, and he laughed. His laugher stopped when he rubbed against her wet panties. Looking into her eyes, he bit his lip. It was her turn to laugh.

"Not this time. You can taste me later. Right now, I need you to fill me. I've been so empty."

"Fuck, that is the sexiest thing anyone has ever said to me."

Once his cock was free of his pants, he yanked her panties to the side, and slid her down his shaft. She was so wet, he slid in all the way without obstruction.

"Holy fuck, you feel so good, Mack."

"This is your show, babydoll. Take what you need. I'm all yours."

The earnestness in his voice drove her, pushed her to ride his cock like her life depended on it. As she got closer, he spurred her on, thrusting up every time she descended. As her release built, tightening her walls around him, he reached between them and rubbed her clit, pushing her over the edge, so he could fall with her.

"You're so damn good, Shar. Perfect. You're fucking perfect." *With each word, he kissed her face and her head, hugging her close. "I don't want you to leave. I want you to stay with me. Let's try this again. If it works, great. If it doesn't, it won't be because we didn't try to get it right."*

Shar didn't even have to think about it. She had no desire to be without him. He was everything she needed.

I have no words. I hear Kassandra in every line. Suddenly the dedication makes sense, and the changes in Shar. My god. I jump up from the couch, and Ferris freaks, clawing at my shirt and simultaneously my chest. "Ow. Shit." I grab him and listen to his tiny complaints. "Sorry. We need to go get your mom, furball."

My phone shows midnight. It's too late to just show up at her house. Would she answer if I text? "What do I do, little guy?" I eye the furry tornado who still looks pissed. I plop back down onto the couch wondering what time she normally wakes up. "We could take her breakfast." Then I remember Louise's comment about some special event at the library. Had she actually taken my advice and set up a signing? Would they have the announcement on the website? They don't say her name, but there is a special event tomorrow from 10am-4pm, and hope warms me from the inside out.

CHAPTER 34
KASSANDRA

The back parking lot of the library is empty when I park as close to the door as I can to carry in the boxes of books. My hands are shaking, and my palms are sweaty, but I refuse to cancel. I need to do this. I'm opening the hatch to start the first trip inside when the librarian brings out a cart.

"Mary, right? You're a gem," I say with the biggest smile I can muster.

"You're the biggest thing this town has ever seen. This is the least I can do."

I turn away toward my books, hoping she doesn't catch the blush that is heating my cheeks. I've not done any in-person events since the stalker from my first book tour. It feels surreal to be preparing for one here.

"Thank you so much for being discreet in your advertisements. I know this was all last minute, but I appreciate it."

"Are you kidding," she said with a huge smile. "It took me nearly a week from your first email to get over the shock, so I could actually respond."

"I'm really not that big of a deal, but someone told me

there were a lot of people on the waitlist for my book. I was both shocked and honored. This is the least I can do."

We get the car unloaded in one trip. Before we get to the door, though, Mary pauses. "Is there a reason you haven't done any events in nearly five years? I'm sure your request for discretion is related, so I didn't want to ask via email."

I sigh. Even knowing the question would eventually come up doesn't make answering it any easier. "When my first book came out, the publishers signed me up for an entire book tour. I wound up with a stalker who went to some significant lengths and money to get close to me. He showed up at signings in multiple states, and even knocked on my hotel room doors. Thankfully, I never traveled or stayed alone. Eventually, he found my apartment and broke in."

"No need to say any more. I'm sorry. I didn't mean for you to have to relive any of that. Stupid nosy brain of mine."

I smile, and she opens the door. There are so many things that time, isolation, and the past month have allowed me to heal from that I am so grateful to be here. My smile holds until we get inside the library proper, and then it grows. She has set up a table in the middle of a large open space and has a line already cordoned off.

"Are you expecting a crowd?" I say with a half chuckle, trying to hide the fact that my heart is racing.

"Small town. News travels fast. Based on the number of people on the waitlist, I expect the whole county might be here by this afternoon."

"Holy shit," I blurt before remembering where I am. "Sorry."

She laughs. "No worries. We just barely opened, and no one is ever here this early on a Saturday. People like to sleep in around here."

I start setting up the table with the newest book and a few copies of previous ones. I even bring copies of Shar's series, except for the last one. I've not hit publish on it yet. Closing my eyes, I make a silent wish about that one. There was no time to order a new banner, so I pulled the one my publishers had created out of the garage. Hopefully, it still opens and isn't rotten, or worse. When everything is as ready as possible, I sit behind the table and wait.

At exactly 10am, the front door opens. I can't see the door from where I'm sitting, but I hear a faint greeting. Moments later, an elderly woman with a walker and a younger woman come walking through the cordoned-off line. The younger woman, her daughter, nurse maybe, covers her mouth with an audible 'oh my god'. I smile as they both pick up the pace to get to my table.

"Good morning," I say.

"Are you really...Is that really..." The younger woman picks up Trials of the Meridien.

"Yes. I write under both M. Knightsong and KM Graham. My name is Kassandra. It's very nice to meet you."

"Oh, dearie," the older woman says with a shaky voice, "if you go through all that trouble to use fake names, don't tell everyone who you are. Give them a fake phone number too. Men don't know how to act."

I laugh and shake her hand. "You are not wrong."

"I'm Marjorie, and this is my mother, Rebecca. We've read the entire Meridien series and are on the waitlist for this last one. Are these for sale?"

"Absolutely, and I'd be glad to sign it for you."

"And this is another one of your books?" Rebecca asks.

"Yes. There are four books in this series. I just finished the last one, but I haven't set a publication date yet."

"Get one of each," Rebecca tells her daughter. "If no one else comes, we'll be the only ones in the whole damn county with all of M. Knightsong's books."

I laugh again and begin signing them. "Thank you both so much for coming out to see me. I wasn't sure anyone would show up."

Marjorie laughs then. "Oh honey, my mother made that statement, but she'll be calling everyone as soon as we get home. If she didn't hate cell phones, she'd be calling them from the car."

No sooner did she finish that statement that the door opened again and then again a half hour later. Gabby and Louise snuck in around 11:30 trying to beat what they called the coming crowd during Louise's lunch break. They weren't kidding. By the time noon rolled around, the door was propped open, and the line wrapped around the library stacks. By 2pm, I had run out of books to sell and had to promise a link to buy more and come back to sign them.

Word must've gotten out about the lack of books because by 3pm, the only people coming have their own copies they had bought previously, mostly from The Meridien series, though quite a few share they ordered the Ms. Independent series as soon as they heard I'd written them too. My heart is so full by the time the line begins to dwindle that I am near bouncing in my seat.

There is still a small line behind the nearest wall of books. Mary comes behind me and whispers that at 3:50, she's going to temporarily lock the library door, so I can finish my line and get a chance to pack up. I thank her silently with a hand on hers that she had placed on my shoulder to get my attention. I can't tell how many people are left, but my energy is fading, so I hope there aren't that many.

A man steps up next and asks me to sign the stack of books in his hand for his wife, Kathryn, who is sick. He claims she sent him home from the hospital to get her books as soon as she heard I was here. I make sure to add well wishes for a speedy recovery. He stands there a little longer than normal, and the hair on my arms start to stand. Please tell me that after this entirely wonderful day, this will not be happening. When I look into his eyes, though, all I see is sadness.

"She might not make it. The doctors are trying everything

they can, but it doesn't look good." The last bit comes out on a bit of a sob, and I jump around the table to hug him.

"I know this is hard. I'm going to send positive thoughts her way for both of you. What hospital is she in?"

"County General. Thank you." He holds me for one more second and then grabs his books and leaves.

I turn to take a sip of my water to keep the tears from crashing. "I'll be right with you," I say over my shoulder to the next person waiting.

"Take all the time you need."

My breath catches, and I have to take a couple of moments before I can turn around and face him. "I wasn't sure you'd come."

He shrugs. "I got this book in the mail, but it wasn't signed. A little kitten told me that if I came today, I might be able to get it signed." He holds out the final Shar book to me at the same time a furry head pops out of his pocket.

"Ferris!"

Asher sighs and hands me the gray bundle of fluff. I nuzzle him.

"I've missed you," I say as I kiss the top of his head. My eyes, however, are on Asher.

"He's missed you too."

"And you?"

"I'm not here for the kitten, Kass."

"No?"

He shakes his head. "I'm here to get my book signed."

I put Ferris on the table and open the book to the dedication page.

Asher McNeil,
You are the Mack to my Shar.
The future is so much brighter with you in it.
I love you.

Kassandra Gingham

"You didn't ask what I wanted it to say."

I give him an uncertain smile. "I hope I got it right."

He opens the book and thumbs through to the dedication page. I watch his face, but his expression doesn't change.

"You don't like it?" I say, my voice tight.

"It's more than I could've hoped for," he says, his voice cracking.

When he looks at me, there are tears in his eyes. He holds out his hand, and I take it. He brings it to his lips and then kisses my wrist before pulling me into him. He is a hair's breadth from kissing me when a squeaky mewl comes from the table at our side. We both laugh.

"That little furry cock blocker," Asher growls against my mouth. I laugh even harder.

"Give him to me."

We both turn to see Louise and Gabby standing by the wall. Louise comes forward and grabs Ferris, nuzzling him to her chin.

"Go. Take your woman home," Gabby says in that gruff voice of hers. I start to protest, looking at the table and my banner. She shakes her head. "We'll clean this up, and Asher can pick it up on Monday." Asher starts to say something, but she stops him. "Boy, don't argue. Git."

He takes my hand and pulls me toward the door. When he turns the truck around in the opposite direction of my house, I ask where we're going.

"My house is closer than yours."

CHAPTER 35
EPILOGUE

Asher tells me to close my eyes before we turn the corner. I don't know what the big surprise is since I saw him working on the plans months ago. Granted, I haven't been to his grandparents' house since because he's told me to stay away, but still.

"Do I really have to keep them closed this whole time?"

"Yes. And if you open them early, I won't spank you tonight."

I laugh, but I keep my eyes closed. "That's hitting below the belt, you know."

"Or not," he retorts, and I can hear the laughter in his voice.

He parks the car and shuts off the engine. "Keep them closed. I'm coming to open the door for you."

I shake my head. He opens my door and grabs my hand, helping me out of the truck by basically bear-hugging me to him. When my feet touch the ground, he turns me until my back is against his chest and covers my eyes with his hands. If I could open them, I'd be rolling my eyes.

"Asher, seriously?"

"Hush, we're almost ready. Don't ruin the surprise."

He leads me about 20 feet in some direction, and then he lets me go. He finally tells me to open my eyes, and he is standing in front of a huge door on a gorgeously modern house. There's no way this is the same house. There are garages on either side of the stairs leading up to the door. The stonework is a beautiful combination of tans and gray with black wood. There are large windows above the door that must let in a ton of light.

"Asher, this is gorgeous. Is this truly the same house?"

His white pearly smile shines in the morning sun. I look around, taking in the full grandeur of the facade. He's done an amazing job, truly. Then I notice two figures standing at the corner of the house.

"Jesse. Malissa! What are you doing here?"

"Asher asked us to come," Malissa responds before Jesse can open his mouth.

"He asked me to videotape your response to the house."

I look back up at my man who shrugs and opens the door, gesturing for me to join him.

"I guess you guys better get in the house, if you want to catch my reactions. The contractor is calling me inside."

By the time we walk through the whole house, I am in awe of his creativity and skills. "The house is amazing, babe. You really have an eye. I love the open concept, the loft, and especially that master shower." I get in close to him and whisper, "I can think of lots of uses for that shower." His smirk sends a thrilling shiver down my spine.

"Yeah, beautiful house, man. Who knew you actually learned something at that college of yours," Jesse says, punching him in the shoulder and then shaking his hand.

"You're going to have people knocking down your door trying to get their houses renovated once they see this." Malissa stands at Jesse's side holding his arm. There's definitely something building between them, and I don't think it'll be much longer before we get a formal announcement.

"Thanks, everyone. Malissa, I sure hope so, else I just wasted all my time and money on this." He opens the hall closet and pulls out a square piece of metal. When he turns it around, my jaw drops. It reads McNeil Construction.

"Oh my god, that's so awesome!" I crash into him and wrap my arms around his neck. "I'm so happy for you. Wow!"

Jesse and Malissa both offer their congratulations, and Jesse is recording again, getting different angles of the sign. Asher looks at me with earnest.

"Kassandra Gingham, you are my muse, and your pursuit of your dreams even after massive disappointment and loss pushed me to want more. I'm glad you love the house because I renovated it with you in mind, hoping you'd be willing to live here with me, well, me and Ferris." He gets down on his knee, and my eyes immediately fill with tears as he pulls out a small box. "Will you meld your story with mine for the rest of our lives?"

I don't even need to look at the ring to know my answer is yes. There is no way I'm letting this man go. I can hardly see him through the tears anyway. When he takes me in his arms, I not only know that I am, in fact, home, I also know the ending to my next book that I'm going to call For the Love of Ferris.

What? It's a much better title than Furry Little Cock Blocker.

LEYA LAYNE

Follow Leya all over social media:
https://linktr.ee/LeyaLayneAuthor

See her website for forthcoming releases and trigger/content
warnings:
https://bisabelwrites.com/leyas-content-is-for-18-only/

Coming Soon
May 2024: The Next #HotHallmark Novel [Still Untitled]

Fall 2024: Falling in Cole County: A Cozy Romance
Anthology